Curry is thicker than water

Stories

JASMINE ANITA YVETTE D'COSTA

BookLand
press

TORONTO, CANADA

Bookland Press Inc.
6021 Yonge Street, Suite 1010
Toronto, Ontario M2M 3W2
www.booklandpress.com

Printed and bound in Canada

Editor: Fraser Sutherland

Library and Archives Canada Cataloguing in Publication

D'Costa, Jasmine Anita Yvette

    Curry is thicker than water : stories / Jasmine Anita Yvette D'Costa.

ISBN 978-0-9783793-9-1

    1. India--Fiction. 2. Humorous stories, Canadian (English).

I. Title.

PS8607.C68C87 2009   C813'.6   C2008-907451-3

*To my mother
who is the queen of my heart*

FOREWORD
BY THE GILLER PRIZE AND COMMONWEALTH WRITERS' PRIZE WINNER
AUSTIN CLARKE

The effulgence of *Curry is Thicker than Water*, Jasmine D'Costa's first collection of stories, is so rewarding to read, so allegorical and at the same time so philosophical, that it heralds the confidence I have in this young writer, who has laid down the geography of a narrative that is so gripping, as it introduces me to the other broad, new ethnicity in Canada's literary landscape; and it is made all the more effulgent by its multi-cultural point of view. It describes a new world and endorses a new year metaphorically and otherwise.

It is also exciting and gratifying to welcome a new writer, who understands how allegory can be used with light-heartedness, and placed for easier understanding on the certainty of a philosophical foundation, that heightens the traditions of culture; and the repudiation of ethnic traditionalism when it is confronted, and indeed threatened, by a modern interpretation of those very traditions.

In "The Elephant on the Highway," the chant and the scream of newness versus tradition, D'Costa shows how a beggar befriends an elephant, equally a beggar, reminiscent of a homeless man in Toronto, and elevates this unusual brotherhood into a scriptural recasting of the philosophy of being "thy brother's keeper." The obligations of this unnatural relationship are humorously displayed and just as seriously fulfilled.

And this comedy rises above the hilarious when we realize that the tragedy of poverty and political structure of officialdom are used as the new vigour, the new way of seeing how poverty can be richer than administrative officialdom.

Curry is Thicker than Water reminding us of the wisdom in the claim that "blood is thicker than water" – this is precisely D'Costa's contention. "Curry," in her new world of realism, is another clever description of the "blood" that runs through the determination and the tactics of the poor and the homeless. It also exposes us to the logic of the woman who protests against pre-arranged marriages and how she can use cleverness to change and outwit the system - and not only change the system of this traditionalism, but peel off the skin that has made this traditionalism no longer relevant in today's multicultural emotional landscape. All this is portrayed against a cultural and neo-religious background of superstition, witchcraft, voodoo and spiritualism. But the way D'Costa describes these natural characteristics of the group, we feel she is talking about a new – and indeed, neo-religious, a new multicultural slab of commandments. The old world of known and tested solutions is juxtaposed in a contest with modernity. The contest is pleasing, is battling, is obliterating the opposition by the way this young author uses satire.

"Eggs" is a story about physical might over sympathy; about the beginning of life; about the symbolism of the egg – to be eaten; to be crushed; to remind us of the fragility of life – of new life. It is also about society's jaundiced attitude towards physical deformity; and the compassionate attitude we ought to have towards the weak. I thought of Humpty-Dumpty on the wall, suffering in his fragility from a fall off the wall itself, so tragic and cataclysmic that "all the king's horses and all the king's men couldn't put Humpty-Dumpty together again." There is a point at which power, wealth, status and the willingness to be violent, cannot prosper.

But how do we explain D'Costa's obsession with landscape; with the political and geographical description of her sensual, tropical landscape in which all her stories are set; and also her narratives of animals and feathered creatures? I insist that she has in mind the primeval classic beginning of the world, the earth, upon which Adam and Eve were placed as tenants. She has therefore described a Garden of Eden, misunderstood in its real usages, now despoiled through the avariciousness of "worldly goods," and laid bare at the rapacious hands of urban development.

The Good Samaritan is visible and voluble in "Two Wives and a Doormat," a story about the abuse of two wives, married, "grabbed in sexuality," by the man to whom they are both married. It is a story about the husband's mental and physical cruelty, which is obliterated by the kindness of a stranger, a woman old enough to be the mother of the two wives, ironically called "Mother," the Good Samaritan. "Mother" is able to bestow this relief to the two wives, only because as a woman of that same culture, a "Mother", she has witnessed – if not experienced - this abuse, herself. "Two Wives and a Doormat" is passionate, sexual, crude, realistic and still compassionate. It is a story of rape and sexual abuse in a society that does not have the same "correctness" of attitude as we are, in this North American world of middle class sensitiveness, regarding our attitude of revulsion to the abuse of women – whether wives, girlfriends, or "partners."

Many women in this world created by D'Costa wish they could resist the parental insistence of pre-arranged marriage; and instead, marry a pumpkin. A pumpkin? No member of her family, father, mother, aunt, uncle, sister and brother can escape under her cynicism and eventual triumph. A pumpkin! More appropriate as an essential base for an appetizing soup than as a partner in bed! But if we understand satire, we see the literal intention of the author to point out the disadvantages of ritual in religious and cultural iron-clad customs. She points out with equal narrative power, the repudiation of this present generation's women, their less traditional religious and cultural rigidity, and their eagerness for a re-evaluation of the traditional presumptions regarding marriages and relationships in marriages.

It could be said that *Curry is Thicker than Water* is a political pamphlet. A protest. But the vein of new literary blood that courses through the narratives in *Curry is Thicker than Water* assures us of the health and the healthiness of Jasmine D'Costa's literary career.

CONTENTS

The sun is no longer a red ball in the now darkening sky. There is just enough light to see his partly naked body with a sari draped around under his armpits and thrown over his shoulders. He stops at the side of the road under the banyan tree with a stone wall around it. The grey stone contrasts against his white "toga" as he corrects the notion of his garment. He sits in lotus position each foot over the top of his thighs unconcerned about the sandal straps that criss-cross up his shins, digging marks into the skin of his legs. His soles, now raised up for all to see, are frayed with the miles of his travel.

A nomadic story-teller has several advantages. He does not belong; he is free and beyond the rules of those he visits. He needs but one story and several languages; his audience is never the same and he depends on the short memory of the listeners.

People gather, ignoring the heat of the day and the grime of the street and the dark clouds that foretell rain. Like the earth they sit upon, deprived of rain, they thirst. They thirst to hear the story they already know from times past, when walking through their shanty homes and mud paths between them, the storyteller stopped to tell his tale.

the elephant on the highway

Vakra tunda mahaakaaya, Surya koti samaprabha
Nirvighnam kuru me deva, sarvu kaaryeshu sarvadaa.

(O God Shri Ganesha of large body, curved trunk, with the brilliance of a million suns, please make all my work free of obstacles – always).

"LET ME TELL you the story of the talking elephant on the Western Express Highway," my nerdy Indian friend Shankar says. "In Bombay."

"Preposterous," I say. "An elephant on the highway? In a city? In Bombay?"

"So you find an elephant on the highway preposterous. Not that the elephant could speak?"

"That, too, of course!"

"I swear," Shankar says, pinching his Adam's Apple as a sign of veracity, "the elephant could speak." My friend is beginning to flush under the brown.

"Hey, hey, my friend, go easy. No offence or anything, but come on..."

"OK, OK," the wiry little guy says, nodding his head in every which way. "You Western guys amaze me. What is unusual about an elephant on the highway? Or cows? Or buffalo? They live in Bombay. Where would they go? What is wrong with co-existence? Anyway, that is neither here nor there."

"Co-existence I understand my friend, we live in Toronto... but really, elephants?"

"I suppose you do not believe that panthers live

in the heart of Bombay?"

"You're taking this too far," I say

"Anyway, Bill," he says, "let me tell you about this elephant."

"Hold on," I say, "let me order another beer."

We sit waiting for the beer while Shankar gears up to tell us this strange story. He's getting animated. Expressive eyes sparkle and we watch him teleport himself to the wonderful land of his birth. I wonder what made him leave it. My inability to relocate to Vancouver for a better job makes the immigration phenomenon incomprehensible to me. Why do it? Apart, of course, from the fact that Canada is the best country in the world and everyone wants to be here?

The beer arrived. Shankar began his story.

I first met Anand when he was a beggar. He begged at the traffic lights at the intersection of the Western Express Highway and Andheri Naka, a few years before they built the flyover. We spent at least twenty minutes each day at the traffic lights waiting to move. I remember the first day Anand ran to my car. "Saab," he pleaded convincingly, "my wife has just died. Her corpse is on the side of the road. I need hundred rupees for her cremation." Tears rolled down and he fell on his knees and said, "I am begging you." He tugged at his hair and then his collar in desperation.

I had just lost my father and I could feel his pain. But, above all, I could not bear the smell that attacked me. I watched with dread the black dirt under his fingernails as he reached for my white shirtsleeves. In a pre-emptive strike, I hurriedly slipped a hundred-rupee note into his hands. He thanked me and said he would never forget my kindness and even went as far as to invoke God's blessings on my unborn children. It was fortunate that the lights changed and I could move on before I broke down from both empathy and the giddy smell that came from him.

I would sometimes see Anand kneeling and sobbing in front of a car drawn up at the traffic lights, but he didn't beg from me again. If I stopped, he folded his hands in a respectful *namaste* and we chatted about the state of the world and the country.

"We would not be so poor if Indira Gandhi was alive," he said. "She had definite plans for us. *Garibi Hatao*! Eradicate Poverty! is no longer the slogan. The politicians do not talk about us anymore," he moaned, shaking his head. At other times we just talked cricket. Whatever he chose to speak about came with grandiose gestures, passionately yet impersonally.

I once asked him how much he made a day.

"On good days I make three thousand rupees."

"Not bad," I thought. Even after bribing the cop on his beat his good days overtook my earnings, not bad at all! It is good to be a beggar. No taxes, good returns... well, almost. I suppose it does not get him shelter. He lives on the pavement. So, you see, my friend Anand, except for no home, makes good money.

Over time he switched over to passengers in taxis because he had run out of cars – they'd become accustomed to the cremation story, and like me had been suckers once.

I knew Anand for several years before I shifted to Toronto. We had bonded and I missed my daily discussions with this most unlikely of friends. It was two years before I could make my first trip home. I vowed to look Anand up on the Highway.

India just hits you smack in the face when you first go back. Jet lag, crowds, people, heat, everything that you did not notice when you actually lived there, suddenly attacks all your senses. Smells, sights, noise… Hey, don't we have five senses?

Shankar counts his fingers and adds, "Yes, touch and taste too! All extreme experiences as you knock against each other at the airport, the roads, and even in the little apartments we live in. I took a taxi a week later after I started to settle in."

This story could go on forever. My Indian friend finds it very difficult to get to the point. I call for another Molson's.

I went to the crossroad but did not see Anand. I got out of the taxi, determined to find his whereabouts, and asked around. The waiter in the restaurant on the corner said, "Didn't you hear the story of Anand and the elephant? Everyone in Bombay knows about him." I said, "No, I have been abroad. Where is he?"

"He lives in the zoo now."

So I took a cab and zipped to Victoria Gardens. It is now called Jijamata Udyan, but I still think of it as the Victoria Gardens of my youth. It was a working day and the zoo was nearly empty of visitors. I found Anand in the elephant stall, rubbing down a sleeping elephant with brush and water. He turned, saw me and ran towards me shouting, "*Bhai saab, bhai saab*, brother, I haven't seen you for a very long time. Where have you been?"

"Abroad. And you I can see have a job!" That's when he told me the story of the talking elephant.

"Ah, I was wondering when, or whether, we would get to that part of the story," I say into my beer, a tad sarcastically. Of course, this is lost on my dear Indian friend.

The elephant had a mahout and lived under the bridge just outside Borivali. The keeper walked him into Bombay through the suburbs and taught him to beg. Both children and adults were always excited to see the elephant, especially watch him beg for cash. They would put a note into the elephant's trunk and the elephant passed it up to the mahout. The elephant was also hired out to more affluent marriage parties to carry the bridegroom.

One day, the elephant was walking down the Highway at Andheri, Anand's begging territory, when he just knelt down on his two front legs, sat, and very slowly lay down, sprawling on his side across the highway, blocking all the lanes going from South to North Bombay. The mahout was distressed. He tried to get the elephant to stand, move, anything, but the elephant just lay there. The Western Express Highway was completely blocked. Cars, motorbikes, and rickshaws were trying to make turns into side streets, causing further chaos. The mahout, realising that nothing could be done, departed the scene. It took a while for the traffic police to come to the spot. They had to walk through the blockage to get to the intersection. A lane on the north-south route was started to ease the congestion.

In the meantime, no one knew what to do with the elephant sprawled on the highway. It was about 8 p.m. Finally, when word went round that the road was blocked, the traffic was diverted. The police summoned a vet from a nearby veterinary clinic. A very reluctant man who had only treated little Pomeranian dogs in his career arrived on the spot. He looked at the animal from a distance, bobbing his head in all directions puzzled. All governmental offices were closed and they did not know under whose jurisdiction the elephant fell. The municipal offices were closed and the forest officers could not be located. "Tomorrow," they thought, "tomorrow someone will decide how to go ahead. Maybe the elephant will just wake up and walk away."

Meanwhile, unconcerned with their dilemma, the elephant lay like dead. That night, Anand, who slept on the sidewalk nearby, walked up to the elephant. He sat on his haunches, curious to see an elephant at such close quarters.

"Sit down with me," the elephant said.

Anand was afraid for his sanity. He had been hearing voices in his head for several weeks now and thought he was going insane. He looked at the elephant and thought he imagined a wink.

"Did you just speak?" he asked him.   The elephant winked. There was no mistaking it now.

"OK, OK. What is all this about? If I am not dreaming or imagining it, are you trying to say something?"

"Oh just sit down," said the elephant. "You have nowhere to go, so what's your problem?"

"I have no problem, but elephants don't talk, you know."

"Who says?" said the elephant.

"Everyone."

"Well, they are wrong. I do talk. You hear me don't you?"

"Yes of course."

"Then sit down."

Anand sat and leaned his back against the front legs of the elephant.

"OK, shoot," Anand said.

"Never say 'shoot' to animals, they don't take it well."

"Sorry, so what did you want to talk about?"

"Everything in general. Nothing in particular. I'm just feeling lonely right now."

"So tell me, are you ill? I mean, can't you get up and go home?"

"Well, I can get up, but where is home? I am fed up with begging. It is time I took a stand, or should I say, I would like to sit this one out."

Anand laughed, slapping his thigh. "Well you are really something, aren't you my friend! You have caused a stir in Bombay. The papers are going to shout tomorrow. You may even make it to the front page."

"I don't care. At this moment I don't care about anything or anybody." The elephant saw Anand's face drop. "Except you, of course. We belong to the same union. Both of us beggars, homeless, scavenging, miserable..."

"Wait a minute, I am not miserable. My name is Anand for a reason. I was always a happy child," getting increasingly irritated at this miserable creature. "And may I inform you that I am not a beggar?"

"Whatever..." said the elephant apathetically, growing uninterested in this deluded man in front of him. He started panting and blowing through his trunk, sending rumbles through the now quiet dark highway, except for the swooshing of the occasional vehicle on the other side of the road.

"What do you mean by *whatever?*" Anand said aggressively, all set to take on this monstrosity in the middle of the highway.

"What is your profession, may I ask?" said the elephant placatingly, knowing full well he might lose the only company he had on the highway.

"I provide a service," Anand said, quite believing what he was now telling the elephant. "People want to believe in their own goodness, and I provide them an opportunity to self-realise. This is no different from a charity or a temple."

"Harrrumph," said the elephant, blowing and rasping and waving his trunk from side to side.

"Don't harrumph me," said Anand, irritated at the elephant's ignorance. "It is a very creative and dignified profession," holding shut the multicoloured striped boxer shorts that flared down like a skirt just above his knees, with all the dignity of a stripper at Sunday Mass.

"Stop all that rasping and blowing hot air into my shorts," he said visibly agitated with this creature, who was cheeky enough to condescend to him. "It is very obtrusive and uncomfortable."

"Now you are objecting to my very breath," said the elephant plaintively. He was dipping further and further into a "Nobody loves me…" mode.

"Don't leeeeve," he pleaded pulling at Anand's shirt with his trunk, as he made ready to go.

"OK, OK, but I need to buy my food," Anand said, "I will be back, let go of my shirt. I don't have many you know." Anand was quite disgusted with this pathetic creature who, if truth be told, was pulling him down in more ways than one. He ran off in the direction of Jogeshwari, making haste to get away from the depressed animal.

And so it was that when Anand returned the elephant lay as if dead with his trunk in a coil.

"Hey, hey," said Anand, putting down the *vadas* he had just bought and pushing on the tusk of the elephant. "Don't hold your breath!" he shouted. "You are getting bloated and blue."

The elephant opened one eye, "Get off my tooth. It is all I have. And stop calling me names."

"?" Anand gestured.

"Well, in case you noticed, or understood elephants, you would know that I am not bloated but the normal size of an elephant. Surprising, considering I go hungry most of the time! And blue-grey is the colour I was born with."

"When I saw your trunk in a coil I thought you were dying or dead. As children, we put salt on earthworms and they curled up like your trunk and died."

"Oh, God!" The elephant groaned. "Can't I ever get it right? I was breathing through my forehead since you objected to my nasal passages. I am hungry and thirsty. Damn this weather! What have you there?"

"This is too little for us both...Oh, whatever..." said Anand, as the elephant started rasping once again and put a *vada* in the elephant's mouth and then another.

They sat companionably through their meal. The elephant didn't think it was much of meal but he was used to abstinence. He looked pityingly at Anand's satisfied face. "What a loser! Look at his lunch, and he is insulted when I call him miserable. A miserable loser," he repeated, careful not to voice the thought.

"Come, come Shankar," I say, "Give me a break. How do you know what the elephant was thinking?"

"Precisely, Bill" Shankar says, "my question too. But Anand said that when an elephant is disdainful, you have no doubt about it. Its eyebrows go up and its eyeballs drop down — a feat I have tried hard to achieve in front of my mirror — making it look like a high society bitch who looks down disdainfully at the Value Village outfit of her personal assistant."

All this is said in one long breathless sentence. "OK," I say, "let's not split hairs. This calls for another beer." I know that my nerdy Indian friend is on a roll.

I get Shankar to sit down. He'd been on his feet, flailing his arms and telling the story and making a spectacle. By now, four tables around us had adjusted their chairs and were intently following the story. Shankar, of course unembarrassed and unconscious of all the attention, stuck his nose into his shoulder and waved his hand back and forth imitating the trunk of the elephant.

"Go on," I say apologetically. "I just need to understand it all. I have never seen an elephant except on TV."

Shankar waves a dismissing hand and carries on.

"Hissss," he whistles through the gap in his front teeth.

"What now pal? You don't say a snake walks into the scene?"

Anand felt the body of the elephant he was leaning against heave, rumble, and then give a hearty shiver. One of the hind legs of the elephant lifted.

"Hisssss."

"What's happening?" Anand asked.

The elephant's eyebrows dropped inches and the freckled pink patch under his ears started to change to a darker hue.

"Not me," he said.

"Now, believe it or not, elephants can blush with embarrassment," says Shankar, who is so carried away with his narrative he's forgotten that all this was happening in the darkness of the night. "Because of the potato dumplings that Anand fed him, the elephant farted."

Shankar makes the event graphic, holding his nose and pronouncing "fart" with a nasal tone, stretching it to "fahrnt."

The woman two tables over to the right pushes away her food and calls for the check. Amazingly, he's conjured up visions of a hole being punched in the ozone layer by a gaseous wind blown by the backside of a three-ton animal on the lonely highway night.

"Take it easy, brother," said Anand to the elephant. "This is disgusting!"

"Fuck this body and all its functions," said the elephant, again curling his trunk into a coil. "I am sick of this life."

"Hey, what's wrong with your life? You just walk around and every one is thrilled to see you. You should see the awe on the *firang* faces when they see you. They photograph you and when they go home to wherever they come from, I bet you are the highlight of their trip."

"I hate it. The indignity of begging gets to me. Walking around indeed! Look at my blistered feet. The hot tarred roads are not for me."

"Well, at least you are looked after."

"And so one would think. Do you know how insulting it is to beg? They put ten rupees in my trunk and I pass it on to the mahout."

"What insults you, the begging or the ten rupees?"

"Both. Begging. Ten rupees. Both make me feel cheap."

"What do you plan to do now?" Anand asked, trying to distract the elephant's new downward slide, feeling dragged down himself. "You know you cannot lie here much longer, don't you?"

"Why not?"

"You cannot affect the traffic. They will find a way to get you off. It might just be a fatal option for you."

"I don't care," said the elephant, "nobody loves me. Look at that cow on the crossroads. She sits there like she owns it and no one seems to object. I barely sit down for a day and they have to get rid of me"

The pair watched the traffic steer around the cow and drive on the opposite side of the highway. The busy Western Express Highway was now slowing down. The traffic had been diverted.

"I hate her," he said unreasonably, banging his trunk on the road. "What is it about that scrawny animal that protects her? Why not me?"

"Hindus worship the cow."

"I have seen them worship the elephant god, Ganesha. So why not me?"

"Ganesha is half-man, half-elephant. You are full elephant," Anand reminded him. "Besides, devotees pray to Ganesha to remove obstacles and my friend, you must agree that at present you are one big obstacle on the highway."

"I want to die," he said.

"Why?" Anand wasn't able to grasp where all this anguish was coming from.

"My life sucks. Besides, I am a full-grown virgin," he groaned.

"No sex? Ah, that explains it."

"None. How about you?" the elephant pouted, if it was possible for the already drooping lips to pout.

"Under the stars," said Anand, nonchalantly.

"With who — yourself?" said the elephant surprised, seeing no partner around.

"Hey, no need to be insulting — the woman

under the bridge," said Anand reluctantly.

"That retard?" said the elephant, unconcerned about a politically incorrect term for the mentally challenged.

"Gosh, how does such a thing happen? Does she have a choice?" I ask Shankar.

"She does not know better. She likes to be screwed. Most of the street men go to her."

"What if she got pregnant?" I ask with an internal shudder.

"She did get pregnant once. The municipal doctors aborted the child, sterilized her and let her back on the street where she lived."

"Boy! It's good to be Canadian! All this seems alien to me. But then much of this story seems alien to me."

Anyway, they both fell silent, each pondering their respective sexual lives — or lack of it.

Early the next day, the morning parade with tin pots of water started. As they gathered outside the wall of the factory for their morning ablutions, they saw the strangest sight — the elephant asleep with his trunk curled into a coil and Anand, the regular beggar on the intersection, sleeping with his head resting on the front legs of the elephant.

By 8 a.m. there was a furore. The Municipal Councillor of Andheri came with a contingent in tow. He had spent much of the previous night on the phone with the Municipal Commissioner. The Commissioner had been unreasonably irritated and the conversation ended with him demanding a report along with a recommendation. The Municipal Councillor, aware that the hard decisions were left to him, called in the vet from the zoo to assess whether the animal should be put down. The animal activists were rallying. They had spent their night making banners and placards: "Save the elephant," "*Hathi mere Sathi*," "Don't let Appu die."

"So was the elephant named Appu?" I ask.

"Oh no! Appu was the mascot elephant at the Asian Games in New Delhi. Everyone links the name Appu with elephants. The Asian Games in India gave great pride for every Indian, so they just used the name to evoke the emotion." Shankar is now quietly drinking his beer.

We all fall in with his mood and wait in silence. After a while he shakes his head, "Incredible! Incredible, the activity on the highway, the next day!" he says, hitting his forehead with the palm of his hand.

"Hey, man, you'll hurt yourself," I say.

Shankar may be nerdy but he sure has an unintelligent way of not listening.

"Incredible," he says, hitting his forehead again and shaking his head from side to side like a wooden Japanese doll with its head on a spring.

His eyes take on a distant look.

Here was the elephant on the highway, immovable, but the bustle around him was like mushrooms springing up in all shapes, sizes, and species. Two schools nearby had the older children on a walking tour to see the elephant. They walked in silence. The teachers kept order with large long rulers.

"Walk in single file!" they shouted, trying to be heard above the cacophony. The children walked, awed and delighted, around the sleeping elephant and exited on the other side of the highway, which by now only the very foolish or optimistic of drivers were attempting.

One of the teachers was a sumo-wrestler-like woman, wearing a box-pleated skirt that ended just below her knees. The pleats spanned open at the curve of her bottom. She had topped it with a white short-sleeved shirt. The shirtsleeves were rolled up further, revealing flabby limbs only rivalled by the elephant's. Ms. Tareporewala, who was banging her thirty-six inch ruler on the street, shouted, "Stop giggling, walk in single file, stop giggling, walk in single...!"

The Chief Forest Officer, Mr. Bhupen, who had arrived fifteen minutes earlier with his assistant, was in deep discussion with the Municipal Councillor of Andheri on strategies to deal with the animal. He kept glancing at Ms. Tareporewala, occasionally frowning at the rapping of her ruler on the street, seeing her as a potential aggravation to what seemed like a very sick animal.

He turned and looked down at his assistant standing behind him. I say "looked down," because though Mr. Bhupen was of average height, his assistant was a short puny little chap who looked like the most unlikely candidate to be on top of the food chain in the forest he worked in.

"Get that woman to stop that," he ordered, "the animal does not need this aggravation. And anyway, what school is this? Why are the children on the highway and not in the classroom?" He turned back to the Muncipal Councillor in helpless irritation.

Ms. Taraporewala was now looking down at the assistant, who was trying to convey the request of the Chief Forest Officer. Her legs apart, her right hand continued to bang the ruler on the street as if a metronome keeping time with her belligerence.

"Do you have any idea how wild those children can get if not tamed?" she asked, waving her free arm way above her shoulders.

Not as wild as the panthers in the Borivali National Park the assistant worked in, but he refrained from comment and walked back gingerly to his position behind Mr. Bhupen.

"Listen, mate," I say to Shankar, "you are pushing your own take on what people are thinking. You are beginning to lose credibility."

Shankar looks at me, not ready to reply to petty objections, and says, "I am only telling you what Anand told me."

Fifty meters away was another world of activity. Swami Maha Ananda Coorswamy Mahadevata Amman Poojari had made a declaration. Lord Ganesha was angry. This was a bad omen. Only pregnant women could save Bombay from the wrath that was soon to strike the city. Pregnant women from various parts of the city were standing in a long queue outside the temple, in their hands *diyas*, little cup-like oil lamps. The bells of the temple were constantly ringing as each crossed the threshold with their offerings. When the local reporter was finally able to get to the holy man for an interview, he denied it with contempt. "I am being set up," he said. "It would be preposterous to get pregnant women out to the temple in these conditions." Nevertheless, pregnant women streamed in with *diyas* in one hand and offerings of sugar in the other. "Just in case," one of them said when questioned by the reporter.

The traffic police were now directing the queue outside the temple.

Another queue formed near the mouth of the elephant. Citizens were queuing with lumps of jaggery and fresh vegetables. Some of them had brought branches and leaves that they had collected along the streets and from trees nearer to their homes and were laying it near the elephant's mouth. The elephant, whose hunger had reached proportions beyond shame or dignity, was gorging on the offerings, still lying on his side.

Standing apart at the top end of the elephant's head, a team of vets who had been called in from the zoo and the veterinary hospital at Parel were deep in discussion about what ailed the elephant. They agreed that whatever the malaise was, it had not affected its appetite. They decided to go to the nearby Udupi restaurant and discuss the matter in more detail over a cup of chai and a masala dosa.

Intense commerce took place at intervals where trees lined the highway. The rain trees and low-spreading gul mohars were being de-branched by street kids and sold to those who wanted to feed the elephant. Hawkers had pushed their carts and were selling *vadas* and tea to the long queues that had lined up to do it.

The elephant, who had been eating unashamedly, now lifted its trunk to the sky and gave a loud burp quite unlike anything they had heard. A loud cheer went up at the first sign of what they thought was a satisfied elephant. The trunk then lowered and was gently placed in the ear of Anand, who was standing by the front feet quite unnoticed. He whispered, "Water! I am hot and thirsty, I need water!"

The crowd gasped. Though they could not hear him, they were struck by the connection he was making with the beggar.

Anand raised his hands, "Water! The elephant needs water. *Pani, Pani*," he yelled, "Lots of water, lots of water. Water on its body, water to drink."

This caused a big commotion. Bystanders and

the animal rights protesters ran in all directions to get a bucket and water. The news travelled down the food line. Those who were further down the line ran to shops nearby and borrowed buckets. They were filling buckets at various shops and now forming a water-relay team. A bucket of water was passed up to the front of the line and a second line was forming to return it to the supply.

The Councillor looked around helplessly. The police walked up and down, keeping the lines in order.

The Councillor turned to the Forest Officer. "Where are the vets?"

The Forest Officer turned around to his assistant, "Find the vets," he ordered.

The assistant, who had been enviously watching the vets go to the Udupi Restaurant, joined the vets to drink chai.

The Councillor, who found the entire situation move completely out of his control, walked up to the Police Inspector, who sat in his jeep silently watching the spectacle.

"Get that woman and those children off this street!" He pointed to Ms. Taraporewala. At least this was something he could control.

The Police Inspector sauntered over to her.

"Madam," he said politely, hitting his truncheon on the street in rhythm with her thirty-six-inch ruler.

"Hold on," she said, not looking at him, "Can't you see I am busy?" Turning to a bunch of girls who were giggling, she said, "Silence, walk in line…"

"Madam," he said now raising his voice, irritated at being rebuffed.

"Miss, Miss," said the bunch of girls, "he is talking to you."

"Silence," she said, banging the ruler on the

street. Turning to the Police Inspector and giving him her full attention, she said, "What?"

"This is not safe for the children, and we are clearing the street. Could you please take the children back to the school?"   All this was said in a serious insistent voice to ensure that Ms. Tareporewala heeded. She stared at him for a minute and he outstared her.

"Right about turn!" she ordered like a sergeant, pointing the ruler in the opposite direction.   The schoolchildren swivelled on cue and moved away in single file, followed by Ms. Taraporewala.

"I hope you had a good look," she said loudly to the girls, "because I expect you to go back to class and write an essay." She yelled, "Single file!" to a group of girls who had bunched up.

In the meantime, the activists had made placards with "Cool the Elephant" and were collecting money from the gathered crowd.

Two blocks away on Andheri East, Chatriwala Apartments, faced with a water shortage, had commissioned a tanker to deliver water for the residents. The unfortunate tanker chose this very moment to crawl closer to the elephant on the other side of the high-way. A loud cry came from the animal activists and the crowd ran in the direction of the tanker. The tanker was forced to halt and the driver got out to negotiate with the crowd. He could not get far. Anyway, he was just the driver so he drove up closer to the elephant and used the spare pipe as a conduit.

A bucket of water had arrived at the head of the water relay and placed near the tip of the elephant's trunk.

At this stage Anand stepped up and raised his hands. "Stop in the name of Lord Ganesha," he said. "The elephant has requested I be the only one to wash him down."

As Anand made this declaration, the elephant sucked in water and sprayed it over the crowd. A loud cheer went up. Anand called loudly for a brush to scrub the elephant down. The word "brush" went down the line, like the game "Chinese Whispers" we played when we were kids. Meanwhile, water was sprayed from the tanker on the elephant's body to cool it down. The water queue had mustered a brush, a comb, a bush, a branch and several quite unrelated objects. Anand took the brush.

The Councillor and the Forest Officer were still debating on what to do. New posters and placards were created. "Save the elephant" was the slogan that the animal activists coined. The crowd chanted:

"Save the elephant!"

"Save the elephant!"

The Councillor, whose instinct was to put down the elephant with a lethal injection and dispose off the body, remembered that his father said, "*Hathi mara tho be sava lakh ka hota hai,*" every time he wanted to point out to his children that they could not outwit him. The Councillor could see that kickbacks could come from the operators of the crane, the transport... His eyes gleamed. This elephant would be more valuable dead than alive.

The Forest Officer was moving his head in various directions making it difficult to decide whether he was agreeing or disagreeing with the Councillor.

The tiny scruffy bespectacled animal rights leader, standing not far from this duo, was moved to walk up to the Chief Forest Officer, wave the megaphone at him, and shout, "You cannot put down the animal. From its appetite it is clearly not ill enough to be put down. It is a clear contravention of section

11(1)(b) of the Prevention of Cruelty Act, 1960, *'wilfully and unreasonably administering any injurious substance to an elephant.'"*

I am finding it hard to follow the thread of Shankar's tale, especially when he lapses into Hindu or whatever they speak in India.

"What does it mean? What did the councillor say?"

"It means that even though an elephant is dead it is still worth 125,000 rupees. We use this phrase when a 'has been' scores a point."

"What happened to the mahout?"

The mahout came back the next morning and, seeing the crowd and the officials, he walked to the elephant and tried to get him to stand. The elephant closed his eyes and the leader of the animal activists stalked up to the Chief Forest Officer again.

"Where is the licence for this animal?" he demanded. And without waiting for a reply, "It is your jurisdiction," he shouted over the pandemonium. "Have you inspected the licence of the owner under section 40(2) and 42 in schedule 1 of the Wildlife Protection Act – 1972?"

The Chief Forest Officer, who felt sorely tried by this aggression, tried to ignore him. The animal activist piqued, walked back and used his megaphone to set up the chant once again, with even more fervour,

"Down with the *babus*, save the elephant!"

"Save the elephant!" the crowd chanted.

"What do we want?" he shouted through the megaphone

"We want a live elephant," they chorused.

At this stage, the Councillor, who by now was

feeling the effects of the hot sun and a situation that was beyond him, left in his jeep. The Forest Officer also left, quite forgetting his assistant.

Anand was getting tired of the crowds, and so was the elephant.

The elephant stretched his trunk to Anand's ears and whispered loudly,

"Get rid of this crowd."

Anand walked up to the elephant's ear, lifted it, and whispered, "You ate so much, why can't you fart now?"

"In a moment," said the elephant.

"Don't say it," I plead with Shankar.

"Sorry, Bill, that is exactly what happened."

He lifted his leg and redirected the wind. The crowds scattered. Though they were used to the evening smells of the creek at low tide and the open drains, there was no bearing this. The crowds rushed away, holding their noses. Soon there was only the odd passerby who took a detour when the gas hit.

So once again, for the second night in a row, the elephant settled down to his night out.

"Will be back soon," said Anand.

"Where are you going? Don't leave me alone!" the elephant pleaded.

"Will take a short walk and let the air settle," said Anand.

So the elephant was once again on the highway, alone and pensive. His excitement began to wane and his earlier mood slowly crept back. Anand returned to a pouting elephant.

"What now?" said Anand. "I thought you were happy with all that attention."

"One would think," the elephant's voice came out with a whiny squeal that seemed incongruent with so large a body. "But do you understand what it is like when you lose control of your life?"

"You just think you have lost control, but you have rights, you know. Did you not hear the animal rights guy talk to the Councillor? Section something of some law or the other. They cannot kill you."

The elephant shuddered at the word. A big tear rolled down his eyes.

"Hey, what did I say? Why are you crying?" He had constantly wept on the highway for funds to cremate his dead wife, but the elephant's tears alarmed him.

"What good are rights when you cannot exercise them?"

"The crowd loved you. They will not allow the Councillor to kill you."

"What if they get the police to disperse the crowd? Who will protect me?"

"The crowd will fight against such an action."

"But I could be dead."

"I thought you said you wanted to die yesterday."

"I am afraid to die." The elephant's body was now quaking.

"Well, make up your mind," said Anand.

"You are very insensitive."

"Stop name-calling. One day you want to die, and then not. I am only a man, not a god. How do I know what you mean?"

"Well, when someone says they want to die, they actually mean they are very lonely."

"OK, I get it. They mean 'Look at me! Look at me!'"

"You make everything sound cheap. You are so insensitive!"

"Then maybe I should leave," said Anand, "I am lonely but I don't want to die so I cannot understand you." Anand stood up.

"Don't leeeeeve me," whined the elephant.

Anand was repulsed by this needy side of the elephant. He walked away without looking back.

The elephant began convulsing. Anand did not look back, ignoring the rasping and the thumping of the trunk on the road. He needed a break from this creature who was pulling him down.

After a while Anand walked back, expecting to find the elephant in a calmer mood. He looked down at the road in the distance as he walked towards the spot where he had left the elephant. His heart jolted. The elephant was not there. Though the elephant had annoyed him considerably, he did not expect this sudden feeling in the area, which he was told, was his heart. Anand ran down the road, his heart thundering. Where was the elephant? As he drew nearer, he saw the elephant standing in the shadows on the opposite side of the road.

"What do you think you are doing?" Anand shouted.

The elephant looked coyly and said, "You love me!"

"Shut up!" screamed Anand, angry at the elephant for startling him. The elephant took three steps towards him, stretched, returned to his old spot, and lay down once again. Anand walked to where the elephant had stood and was met with an assault to his senses. Heaped on the other side of the road was tons of 'processed food' the elephant had eaten all day.

"Disgusting," said Anand.

"Don't be dramatic," said the elephant, who ignored his own tendency towards drama. "It is a logical conclusion to the day."

The elephant went back into position. However, having been on one side for more than a day, he decided to lie on the other side.

Anand stood pondering. He had made no money ever since this monster had decided to block the highway. He saw his opportunity now.

"I will be back," he said.

"Where are you going? Don't leave me," the needy creature said.

"Will be back soon."

"Don't leave me, I am afraid to be alone."

"I have to get rid of that pile you created," he said pointing to the dung heap across the highway.

"How?"

"I will sell it to the buffalo stable in Goregaon," Anand said, moving away.

An hour later, he returned with a bullock cart and its owner, who had pledged to pay seven hundred rupees for each cartload of dung. They used spades to load the cart and the cart was driven away.

"Cannot say it was all a loss," said Anand. "Three loads a day — I will be rich!"

"We are talking about my future here, not yours," the elephant reminded him, disgusted at this commerce.

"OK, OK, what do you want... I mean, what do you reallllly want?"

"I want what any elephant wants. A mate, family, love and, above all, the security that they won't be taken away from me. Besides, I know for certain I don't want to go back to my mahout or to beg on the streets. It is so humiliating."

Anand was feeling uneasy. The elephant had touched on everything that Anand did not have.

"We all want that too," he said, "but we don't get it. That is life!"

"But we can dream. Hope is life itself. And if you take that away I just want to die."

"I don't want to take your dreams away, but for now perhaps we need a plan of action. You cannot be lying here any longer or they will surely stick a needle into you and take you away with a crane."

"What can I do?"

"You cannot do anything without knowing what you really want."

"I may not know what I want, but I definitely know what I don't want."

"That is a good start. Let us do it by elimination."

"Help me."

"Do you want to go back to the mahout?"

"Nope."

"Do you want to go to a jungle?"

"What? And live with the wild animals? Certainly not!"

"You could be wild and free too. That is who you are."

"No, that is not who I am. I won't know my way and I don't know how to live there. I would be too afraid to take care of myself."

"Do you want a different mahout?"

"Nope."

"A private owner?"

"Nope."

"A circus?"

"No way. I suffer from stage fright."

"Why do I get the feeling you know what you

want?" said Anand. "Go on then. Say it."

"OK. OK. I want to be in the zoo."

"Well, with this performance you put on, they think you are too ill to be saved. Unless you show them you are well, only a miracle can save you."

"That's it," said the elephant banging the trunk on the street.

"?" Anand spread his arms, looking askance.

"Don't you see?   A miracle! That's the solution."

"You have lost me there, brother."

"You will perform the miracle."

"And will you also tell me how to do that?"

"You are a performer."

"Yes, but not of miracles. I think you have eaten too much and are not thinking straight."

"Maybe you should get into costume."

"Oh yeah? And what kind of costume do you suggest?"

"Saffron."

"Saffron?"

"Oh, find one," the elephant said, impatient with such petty details. "It is a very good plan."

"What *is* the plan?"

At this point, Shankar pushes back into his chair and goes into a reverie. This is most irritating. He has me primed but now we are back again in the bar.

"Go on, Shankar," I urge after a few moments.

"So the next morning there was renewed activity on the highway," he carries on, looking at his wristwatch. "Bill, I think I must leave now, I will tell you the rest tomorrow."

"Shankar, listen, man, this is not the time to walk off."

"Bill, I cannot keep my mother waiting."

"Sit down," I order, pushing my cell phone across the table. "Call her."

Watching Shankar talk to his mother is torture. I watch his black, slightly balding head bow forward, speak in conciliatory tones to his mother, and then put on a high-pitch cooing. It took all of my self-control not to pick the rolled up Metro on the table and smack his head with it. And I am not a violent man!

Several moments later, after more cooing and nodding, he disconnects and leans back meditatively. I pick up the rolled-up newspaper and impatiently tap the table. But our friend is not to be hurried. He stares awhile and finally looks up glassy-eyed.

"The headlines were screaming the next morning, ELEPHANT ORDERED TO DIE." He raises his hands with palms facing outwards from the centre, index fingers and thumbs at right angles.

"You cannot order anyone to die, not even a sick animal," I say.

"Bill," Shankar says, "I don't understand you. There are larger issues at stake here than petty editorial corrections."

I shrink in my corner.

The Municipal Commissioner finally decided. The animal would be tranquilized and taken by crane outside the city, where further action would be determined. The immediate issue was to clear the highway and keep the flow of commerce.

Very early the next day, the activists poured in. The group calling themselves the AA were putting up a makeshift tent of tarpaulin.

"Well, that was nice of Alcoholics Anonymous to come

out to the protest," I interject.

"AA stands for Animal Activists, not Alcoholics Anonymous," said Shankar, a trifle condescendingly. "Anyways, they set up this tent, with a board outside that read FAST UNTO DEATH RELAY."

"Fast unto death relay?" I ask. "What is that?"

"Well they recruit volunteers to fast unto death. They sit under the tent in three-hour shifts."

"Shifts for a fast unto death? How does that work?"

"Even the fasters have a life you know," says Shankar, impatient with my naivety. "They sit in three hour shifts and then go about their lives when the next batch takes over."

"But doesn't fast unto death mean you don't eat till you die or achieve your goal, whichever comes first?"

"No. It is more of a fast while under the tent, till the matter dies!" he says with a hint of a smile.

That was only the beginning. People converged from all sides. Today was the day of reckoning. The vets and the crane were scheduled to arrive at noon. However, from eight a.m. onwards, as the trains drew in at Andheri Station, hordes of people poured out and walked north towards the highway. Many small-business owners, who wanted to be there too, had closed their offices for the day. Buses had been re-routed. People from Saki Naka marched south towards the highway. The police parked their vehicles two hundred meters away from the crossroad. Strangers were bonding on the road to the highway. People took positions to get the best view of the elephant and the expected execution. The tension mounted and a strange excitement took hold.

The leader of the AA was marshalling the crowds

in concentric circles around the elephant to prevent any approach to the creature. He put the megaphone to his lips and announced, "This is our Chipko movement. We shall protect the elephant till we die!"

The vets, meanwhile, refused to come to the spot without police protection. The clock was ticking. The AA group leader kept looking at his watch.

"Brothers and sisters, it is now 11.30. Be prepared."

The elephant was rolling his eyes, looking for Anand. But Anand was nowhere to be seen.

"11.45," announced the AA leader.

A murmur rose from the back of the crowd. Four vets surrounded by armed guards were pushing their way towards the elephant. The crowds parted to let them through. The murmur rose to a frightening crescendo as they got nearer.

"Chipko," the AA leader announced through the megaphone.

On cue, all the front-row protestors hugged the shaking, very scared elephant.

"Where the hell is Anand?" the elephant asked himself.

"Chipko," the megaphone announced once again.

The second line of protestors stepped forward and hugged the first row.

"Chipko."

"Chipko."

"Chipko."

The posse of police and vets slowed down, perplexed.

There was complete silence. The megaphone announced once again,

"Chipko."

From the direction of Jogeshwari a fresh murmur arose. The crowds parted to let through a man dressed in striped shorts with a train of a wedding *mandap* cloth secured in a knot around his neck. He stepped out front in splendid style. Before they had time to react, the elephant stretched his trunk to Anand's ears.

"Where were you?"

Anand ignored this giant blue jelly and stepped forward. He raised his eyes to the sky and, with his arms high above his head and a makeshift cane in one hand — not very unlike Moses parting the Red Sea — he walked up to the elephant.

All eyes were now riveted at him.

The elephant sighed, in both relief and resignation. Anand's idea of a saffron robe was ludicrous, but he was here...

Anand strode confidently up to the AA leader and took away the megaphone from him.

"Listen, in the name of Lord Ganesha, I ask you to listen!" he said.

Amid whispers, the crowd looked interested. Those at the back were trying to get to the front for a closer view. Then the elephant wrapped his trunk around Anand and lifted him in the air. The crowd gasped. Anand, unfazed, was still holding the staff in one hand high above his head and in the other, the megaphone to his mouth.

Very gently, the elephant lowered Anand on his body, providing a raised platform.

Anand's hand with the staff was still in the air. With the megaphone in his other hand raised to his lips, he went on.

"I had a dream," in a voice that rang with an emotion and wonder that Martin Luther King might envy.

"I had a dream," he repeated.

"Lord Ganesha appeared to me in a shining light." At which his eyes glazed over in wonderment and total self-belief. The crowds were struck by his sincerity. The more devout were stricken with emotion.

Anand, who had spent his last few years in dramatic begging on the Highway, was now in no hurry.

"Om," he said.

"Om, Jai Ganesha," he went on, looking around and, like a music conductor, urged the crowd to join in.

"Om, Jai Ganesha," they chorused. Hail Ganesha.

The devout folded their hands in prayer.

"It is Lord Ganesha's command that this elephant be saved."

At this, the crowds let out a loud cheer. Jai Ganesha was heard here and there.

Anand raised his hands once again to signal for silence. A hush fell.

"It is the will of Ganesha that this elephant be married to Savitri, the elephant in the Jijamata Udyan. It is a marriage made in Heaven!"

The crowd cheered, and stopped in mid-march the small coterie of police and vets. Like the others, the police were interested in this spectacle, and stood in suspended animation, surrounded by the crowd, who were no longer paying attention to them.

"So now in the name of Lord Ganesha, I shall heal the animal from its illness and serve him as Ganesha commands!"

The crowd was now holding their breath in wonderment. Could this be? Anand tried to scramble down with regal dignity, tripped over his cloak and slid off the elephant. The crowd chuckled, some of them even a bit ashamed at falling for this apparent charlatan's melodrama.

However, the scorn that some of them felt, was stemmed by what followed this debacle. The elephant, who had been forgotten, picked up Anand and stood him back on his feet very gently. They watched the trunk stretch and link with Anand's ear but missed the elephant's whisper.

"Good performance, my friend," the elephant hissed.

Anand regained his poise and his flowing garment, which had detached from his neck, and secured it. He put a finger in his ear, which very recently had been blown into by the elephant, and shook it in an attempt to stop the vibration. He clapped his hands to get off the dirt of the street where he had fallen, picked up his staff and his dignity and, raising his other hand, stretched the staff across the elephant's body.

"In the name of Lord Ganesha, I command you to rise," he said in the style of the miracle workers who had gone before him.

The crowd gasped in astonishment. The very sick elephant was now rolling over and kneeling. There was a hushed silence. Could it rise? Would it?

The elephant then knelt on its back knees and did a rotating motion with its buttocks, a bit like the Macarena, and stretched its neck muscles in all directions, causing the concerned crowd to fall back.

It stood up on all fours and shook its body. The crowds gasped. This was truly a mighty miracle of Lord Ganesha. The elephant stood upright on its hind legs with the front legs bent at the knees and, raising its trunk to the sky, trumpeted one long blast. The crowd fell back, more in awe than in fear, and the devout had tears in their eyes.

The elephant finally took a bow after this wonderful performance, picked up Anand in a grand gesture, and placed him on his back. Anand, with the megaphone still in his hands, announced, "Onwards march to the zoo."

The elephant began to walk. Behind him came a long procession of all those who had come out to see the spectacle. Cell phones were busy, as people rang their family and friends all over the city. As the elephant marched, the crowds poured in from all over and joined the procession as it made its way through the streets of Bombay.

The vets were lost in the crowds and the police retreated into their jeeps. Calls were flying from the cell phones of the Municipal Councillor and the Forest Officer. Never in the history of the city had paperwork been done with such speed as at this moment (of course, if you are picky about accuracy, paperwork without cronyism or money passing hands)."

Shankar stands up, ready to go. "Bill," he says, "can you give me your phone for a sec?"

"Sure, man," I say, pushing it towards him.

"Amma," he coos. "I am done here. I will be home in ten minutes."

Disgusting, the way he talks to his mother. His voice changes and gets that high pitch.

"Yes, Amma, of course I will be eating dinner with you. Yes, yes, I love your chicken biryani. I will be there in ten minutes."

"Hey, man, that can't be the end of the story. What happens next?"

Dada Thakur, the well known land grabber, the slum

gangster, the encroacher of all encroachers, marched unnoticed with his goons as the triumphal procession disappeared down the highway. They carried a smooth rock, the size of a footstool, painted orange with a white *trishul*, a trident-like object. They laid it down on the pavement at the side of the road, where you can see today a little temple, large enough to collect alms.

And it came to pass, as they say in the Bible, that Savitri the zoo elephant was wed to our own highway elephant.

eggs

Omne vivum ex ovo.
(All life comes from an egg).
~ Roman Proverb

THE MAN LIMPS laboriously up the slope on the edge of the ocean. He sets up his viewing equipment and trains it to the Northeast, over the Atlantic. He has spent a good two years watching the glacier that clings to mother rock with desperate fearful fingers. As he watches its moving contours one of the fingers disentangles. He slowly trains his viewing equipment east, over at the ptarmigans' nest.

He is sure it contains eggs...

To the north of his eyeball the ice moves. A small mound appears over the ridge. It takes few moments for him to see the outline of the fox's head. As it disappears, white on white, the tell-tale dark blue shadow on the snow moves stealthily forward. Absolutely! He nods his head up and down. Most definitely has eggs. The ptarmigan flaps her wings and lifts at the stealthy onward movement. The fox walks boldly over to the nest and dips his nose into it. The Man squints through the lens and watches the fox beside the nest lick his chops.

Like every other day after the monsoons, the sparrows doze in a line on the telephone wires, high above the verdant paddy fields. The palm trees stand in reverential silence in the still air, almost afraid to rustle their leaves. The bunds, on the side of the paddy fields, elevate them beyond reality. The sunshine feels moist, languishing, susegado! This is Goa, a tropical haven that gently eases the slopes of the Western Ghats into the Arabian sea. The churches, chapels in fields and on the sides of the roads and the old stately bungalows are a reminder of the not so long ago Portuguese rule. But that is not all the Portuguese left behind. In no other part of India is the indolent afternoon siesta so religiously followed.

It is exactly one p.m. Children stream out of the two schools in the centre of Margao. The synchronized sound of shutters hit the town as shopkeepers pull them down. It is the last sound here till four p.m. Francis pulls out his bike from the stand in the corner of the school playground and swings his right leg over it. He lets the cycle roll down the slope from the school to the bus terminus and picks up speed, winds through traffic and cycles past the garden in the centre of the town. Nothing feels more powerful than riding his bicycle. No one notices his clubfoot. He turns left and makes his way home down the road to Santemol Raia.

The little village of Santemol Raia sits silently between Rachol and Margao, in South Goa. As he pedals past the vast hill of garbage, dumped by the City of Margao, at Sonsodo, Francis feels the stinging tears cloud his vision. The smells from the dump hiss through the smoke of acrid little fires that are almost invisible in the bright sunlight. He wipes his eyes with his sleeve distractedly, and labours up the slope.

Francis stopped smiling when he was six. The other boys did not want to play with him. It just dawned on him that limping was not normal, in fact, even shameful. As he hobbled past the booing kids, he tripped over the outstretched leg and hit the ground face first. He lifted himself with as much dignity he could muster and limped away; his upright back belied his defeated eyes gushing rivulets of tears that streaked through the mud banks of his face. No indeed, limping was not normal.

Francis stopped smiling.

Perpetua searched for her little boy, the smiling child she had nursed. She looked at this sombre little stranger and felt a pang. Two months later, she went out and bought him a tricycle.

His head at a forty-five degree angle and hands trying to steady the swaying bicycle, he watches the sea eagle glide just over the top of the hill. She hovers in the distance. Her wings, perpendicular to her body, white flanked with black, gleam in the afternoon sun. He can feel his heartbeat. As sure as he is of anything, Francis is sure: the eagles are back!

He stops at the top of the hill and hides his bicycle in a bush on the roadside. This is disputed land that the *Communidade* and the Church claim as theirs. The wood trees, choked by the wild bushes and creepers, push heavenward gasping for air in their abandonment. Impenetrable... or so it seems to the odd passer-by; twenty meters inside, the dark growth suddenly drops down into a ravine and bursts into a little pond at the bottom. Only the quiet slow rustle of the krait, through the dried leaves, twigs and moss, disturbs the solitude. Francis creeps with familiar confidence through the underbrush. This is his arbour, shared with the bush gnome and his strange little friendly family. He talks to them, plays with them and on occasion fights with them. They laugh with him when he is happy and wipe his tears when he cries. He knows all about this place. He knows the eagles are back; he knows where they are nesting.

He comes to a slight opening where the nest sits on a crag, exactly like it did three years ago. Three meters of confused twigs and leaves, balance close to the edge of the cliff, daring gravity and the winds. Francis watches, breathless, as the large eagle twists in the spot and knows in a flash there are eggs hidden atop the plateau of dried leaves, twigs and fresh green leaves.

The eagles disappeared three years ago after he stole their eggs. He put the eggs in paddy till they hatched. At fourteen he became the proud parent of two beautiful eagles. All his friends looked at him with new interest, even respect. Every morning the residents of Bella Vista in Santemol Raia opened their door to an earnest boy with a pail to collect their fish entrails.

The chicks were soon little black and white patchwork fledglings ready to take off. He named them Tina and Sean and loved them more than he had loved anybody in his young life. They could soar and fly and his limp did not matter to them. They were his: they were his babies.

He sits back, his bottom on the floor of the hill, cross-legged and silent. He tries not to move, ignoring the tears streaming down his cheek, as they tickle his chin. He watches the eagle and gulps with pain as images of Tina and Sean flash through his mind. The eagle spreads its wings, hovers, ready to fly. She sees

Francis in the bush. She flies up into a tree and watches him— unflinching

Francis watches the sea eagle and knows he must leave. He creeps back to the road, where his bicycle lies hidden in the underbrush. He sits erect on his cycle, as it rolls down the other side of the slope and turns on the corner of Bella Vista. He takes the first lane on the left towards his home, dodging the pigs on the street by sheer instinct and rides through the silence around him till he reaches the end of the cul-de-sac. The low drone of his mother praying loudly inside makes him wince. He pushes the gate open and drops his bicycle at the entrance. The sharp smells of fish curry are heavy in the living room.

He looks at his mother, rosary in hand and her little pup in her lap, sitting in front of the altar. He hates her; so false, she could have treated his clubfoot as a child. Maybe he would not have to limp... He winces. She is cruel, wicked and ignorant and I hope those are prayers for forgiveness...though I cannot forgive her. Liar too... She told him that Sean and Tina had flown away. The neighbours saw her bury them in the backyard. Wonder if I am really her son...

The bright red beetle stood frozen, unblinking. Advancing threateningly towards her was a giant hen, wings flapping and clucking deafeningly. With one eye on the monster and the other desperately heavenward, she wept:

"Help me, if indeed you exist."

Suddenly her sky went silent and dark red. Then what seemed like a black hole parted the red slowly from a thin black vent into a round red-rimmed black hole. 'Is this what the red sea looked like, when Moses parted it...or perhaps the birth of a planet?' thought the beetle inconsequentially, overpowered by the gaseous smell. She watched fascinated, convinced she was now watching a miracle, convinced it was the birth of a planet; she watched unblinkingly as the brown smooth surface filled the black hole. Within seconds that seemed like a lifetime, she watched the large smooth brown world stand erect in front of her.

The athletic, dull rust-colour hen looked into the distance dreamily. She ambled slowly, her head bobbing like a Japanese spring doll. As she shook her bottom and tried to adjust the stretched muscle, one of the two circling eagles swooped down and picked her up, heavenward... The little red beetle closed her eyes, overcome. God's own angels had flown down and saved her.

Minutes later, Perpetua opened her door to very angry knocking.

"Your eagles s-s-stole my hen." Vasco stammered.

"God, why are you trying me?" she said to herself.

"Our eagles?" she said, trying to look surprised.

"Y-Y-Yes. Y-Y-our e-e-agles."

"How do you know they were our eagles?" she said, as she dropped the broom on top of the tell-tale pile of rust feathers.

"D-D-ont play with me. Your eagles have terrorized the village for the last two years. I have complained to the Sarpanch. That was our C-Christmas..." he stopped, unable to continue as his sobs racked him.

Perpetua was shocked. She had never seen a grown man cry. It was common knowledge in the village that Vasco was barely able to support his five children. She began to panic. Her own visions of Christmas were dismal. She had overshot her budget for the month and now this...

She put her hand inside her neckline and pulled out a twenty-rupee note from the depths of her bra, and handed it to him. The Eagles had to go...That day, she poisoned the fish entrails Francis had collected from the neighbours to feed Sean and Tina.

"Francis *putha*, my son, I cooked mackerel curry and rice, serve yourself. I fried the fish eggs separately for you."

Perpetua can feel his hatred and is sure he knows about the birds. They had become a nuisance in the village. They were very unlike wild birds and never flew too far to hunt. They hovered over the village; stole from the fish baskets of the small fisher folk in the open fish market at Santemol; sat on roofs around the village; swooped on children eating outdoors; took pickings from the village folk. The people were alarmed and scared for their children. They felt terrorized by the two birds and had complained several times to the *Sarpanch*. Vasco was the last straw... Yes I was right...I am right.

Perpetua looks back at her son and catches his look of hatred. She sighs. He knows. Of course, he knows. He looks away – unable to look at her without the rush of anger.

The return of the eagles is a sign. It is time for retribution.

A week later on the morning of September 19, 2005, Perpetua and the other women from the village gather at the cross road of Bella Vista and the road to Rachol to go to Batim. In 1995, a hair stylist from Canada claimed to see apparitions of the Blessed Virgin Mary at Batim. It was widely reported by the press and ever since, on the 13th of September, October and November, Batim is overrun with devotees of every religion, hoping for a miracle. Perpetua never misses any of these excursions. She spends hours on novenas and every possible promise of hope, imploring the Virgin to help her with her finances. Only a miracle will work. Mary Blessed Virgin, if ever there is someone out there who will help us, please send him to us.

Francis watches her walk to the bus stop at the junction. He peers through the compound of the neighbour opposite their house and waits for the buzz of 'Hail Mary, Full of Grace...' to go by. He dresses up slowly, one foot on the floor as he hops to put his leg into the trouser. Still pulling up his pants, he hops to Perpetua's bedroom. There is a tiny whimper from her pup that she has put in a carton, with a mattress made up of old clothes. He zips up his pants, picks up the pup and puts it in a polythene carry bag – with the legend "Uncle's Kitchen" printed on it – from the restaurant near the Chapel.

He limps unhurriedly to the stone wall at the end of the cul-de-sac and swings the bag against the wall. He hears a loud yelp; he repeats the motion till there is no sound any more.

He slings the bag on his bicycle handlebars, pushes his bike and jumps on the seat. It is a laborious ride up the hill but he does not notice it. His mind is on the nest. He hides his bike in the underbrush, takes the polythene carry bag with him, and creeps silently towards the nest. The birds are not there. He climbs over the nest. Bingo! Two eggs gleam in the bright sunlight. He is quick; he takes the eggs, puts them gently on the floor beside him, and then empties the offering he has brought for the birds.

Placing the eggs very carefully in the bloody polythene bag, he hobbles hurriedly back to the road and fills the bag with leaves, to pad the eggs. He gently hangs the bag on the handlebars and mounts his bicycle. It rolls easily down the slope. Mindful of his booty, he rides home carefully.

Perpetua spends the next two days searching for her pup. It is nowhere to be found; but she finds two eggs sitting in a shoebox, under Francis's bed. Not again! She boils water and put the eggs in for a good ten minutes. She takes the eggs, places them back in the shoebox and pushes it under the bed.

The Man hobbles down waving his hands in mindless signalling as he watches the last finger that holds the glacier to mother rock disengage. The glacier drifts speedily away to sea - like a little white boat, steered by what seems like a fox with his paw in a ptarmigan's nest.

two wives and a doormat

*The Vedanta recognizes no sin, it only recognizes error.
And the greatest error, says the Vedanta is to say that you
are weak, that you are a sinner, a miserable creature, and
that you have no power and you cannot do this and that.*

~ *Swami Vivekanand*

SHE BENDS OVER, clutching at her crotch. I watch her sitting in the shadow at the other end of the room, her face averted, and feel a mixture of anger and jealousy. Her hair in long loose strands down her back makes it difficult for me to see her face. She turns and, in that instant, I could only pity her.

Her hands, palm over palm, are tightly clutched between her thighs and her confused eyes are wet. Is she crying? It is then I see how young and vulnerable she looks. It is only then I understand that this was her first time and she did not enjoy last night with my husband.

Why do I say, "*my* husband"? He is married to *both* of us.

Looking at her frail young body, and sensing her revulsion of the night, I feel only pity and a strange maternal feeling creeps up somewhere in my chest. I go to her, sit behind her and let her lean her head on me. We sit like that in silence for a long while till I take the comb and start running it through the dishevelled hair. I put coconut oil to help me comb the matted hair smoothly and then turn her towards me.

In silence we sit, she and I, as I part her hair in the centre. Very slowly and very gently, I braid two separate locks into plaits. She looks much younger now. What was she? Sixteen? Fifteen? Who knows! I do not know how old I am either. Sometimes I feel very old. Nearly thirty! I may even be thirty. Who knows! But look at her now. She lays her head on my lap like a little child and I notice the red stain on her dress where minutes ago her palms had pushed.

I help her up, wash and dress her. We both sit in silence — I, with my basket of jasmine flowers that I begin to weave into a *veni*, flower garlands to adorn hair, while she sits besides me interested and more animated than I had seen her an hour ago. I give her a piece of twine and show her how to weave the flowers into a long garland. I need to finish the basket for today. She is a good learner and at the end of the hour she makes her own *venis*.

We sit peacefully with this task occupying our hands. While our minds..? At least I know mine is occupied with, *what is she thinking*? I see a fleeting fear as she looks at me occasionally and I know she dreads the return of Him, our husband. What a difference between the two of us. I want to be ravished and she? She is frightened. And Him? He is too drunk to know whom he sleeps with.

He came home last night with this petite girl.

"I married her," he said, "You had your chance to give me a child but you did not. This is my Hindu right to take another wife to get a son."

"That is because you fall asleep on my body," I told him.

He raised his hand to strike me. I ducked and walked away.

"Serve us food," he ordered.

I served one thali and they both ate out of it.

Yesterday I hated her. But today, oddly enough, I pity her. I even want to mother her, protect her. I hold her close to me till she falls asleep in my arms. I lay her down on the mat and get on with making dinner. She is still asleep as I sit on the doorstep watching the people from the big buildings walk by.

I wait for Mother. She walks by holding her husband's hand every day at around six. They always look so calm and peaceful. I do not know her name, I just call her Mother. She lives in the tall building, a block from our transit camp. I sit here each day to watch her pass. She always nods at me and smiles in greeting. I have not seen her for a week.

Today she is alone. She nods and says,

"*Beti*, daughter, how are you? You look unhappy."

I smile. I am excited. This is the first time she talks to me and she calls me *beti*. I wonder how she knows I call her "Mother" in my mind, or how much I long to be her daughter, her real *beti*.

"I am fine," I tell her. "Where is Uncle?"

"He is not well," she says as she keeps walking on. I look at her lovingly.

She is so kind and talks to me even though she lives in one of those big buildings, while I sit here in our one room tenement, illiterate and poor.

I continue to sit here staring out into the evening, watching those that pass by my doorstep. They walk on as if I am invisible. And I watch the dogs as they lift their legs and urinate around the Bombay street I live on and form a gang, ready to attack any other stray dog from another gang. The gang always barks when they see Him. I know He is coming from a mile away. Sheila now awakens and sits by my side in silence - waiting

We hear the dogs bark, rise together as if on cue, and go indoors. I pretend to cook while she sits huddled in the corner. He enters swaggering. If a drunken man can swagger, He does.

"*Rand*, whore!" he yells, unmindful that the sounds carry through the thin walls to the neighbours tenement. "What did you earn today?"

"Nothing," I say defiantly, ducking to dodge his slipper, which he throws across the room. He then turns around and sees the silent figure of Sheila huddled in the corner. It's as if fear turns him on. I can see him swell and know I will have to watch them once again. I turn away, ashamed of my own need . As he pulls off her skirt and stands over her undressing, I sit in the corner, touching my nipples that have hardened now. I watch her naked breast as she turns and walks to the centre of the room and lies down waiting for him. The streetlight shows her bare body and his as he pumps away. I feel the twitch between my own legs and slowly watch them as I masturbate in the corner. He is finished as soon as he starts and turns over, panting, while she clutches her crotch again.

Take me, my mind screams, as I continue to masturbate and feel the electricity run through me. He starts snoring and she runs to me as I come with a shudder. She hugs me in fear as I hug her, as I would have hugged any body in front of me in that wild moment. We sit in silence while I cradle her in my arms and gently rock her to sleep.

He rolls over and sits up, rubbing his eyes. Then he gets up, walks to the front door and pushes it open with his left hand while his right hand holds his penis. He stands and pisses on the road and on the three doorsteps.

As he turns and sees me awake, he is once more aroused. He walks over to me, sits down on the floor a meter away and pulls my ankles, drawing me down.

I am ashamed. I hate this man who my parents arranged for me and yet I can feel the wetness between my thighs. Within seconds, it is over, leaving me crying, wanting more, and as he turns and falls asleep almost at once I rub myself to sleep.

The morning brings with it much shame. I see her innocent little body lying there and his grossness besides us. I know he will soon wake and take our earnings of the day. I keep it out there in the open so that he does not find the money I hide in the pressure cooker on the shelf. He wakes up and stands at the doorway, tracing a pattern on the road with his piss. He walks in, changes his clothes, grabs the money on the counter, puts it inside his shirt pocket and walks out wordlessly.

We sit together, Sheila and I, weaving flowers in silence. After we finish, I go down to the bazaar road, where I deliver to the flower stall and take the cash and a fresh load of flowers. As I hurry home, I look at the woman on the corner begging for food: it terrifies me. What if he throws me out now that he has a new wife? I rush home. Sheila is animated. "I cooked rice," she says, bobbing up and down like a child. I look at her, wondering what to do. I must think. I sit in the fading light on the doorstep waiting for Mother to pass. The threshold is too narrow for both of us to sit and Sheila kneels behind me with her arms around my neck, peering out into the road.

Mother comes at her usual time and smiles at us.

"Is this your sister?" she asks.

"No, He married her."

She looks shocked, but says nothing and starts walking on her way. I push Sheila's arms away and run behind her.

"*Mataji*, can you help me?"

"How?" she asks.

"Wait here," I tell her and run back indoors. I take the hundred rupees from the pressure cooker and hand it to her.

"*Mataji*, can you keep this for me? He takes all my money and if he finds this he will throw me out, now that she is here."

Sheila looks scared. She had followed me and was standing behind me.

"*Didi*, I cannot stay with Him alone."

Mother looks at us for a long while and then at the hundred rupee-note.

"Do you have a photograph?" she asks.

"No," I say.

"Tomorrow morning come to my building gate at ten," she says and I nod.

I tell Sheila not to say anything to anyone. She nods. I sit with the flowers and weave. I have to deliver it before nine a.m. or else I will not be able to meet Mother. I wonder what she will do for me. I wonder why she wants my photograph. Sheila sits at the doorstep, waiting. We listen with one ear for the barking of the dogs signalling Him. We do not know what He does during the day. We do not want to know. He enters today already swollen. He grabs Sheila. I sit with the basket of flowers turned away from him, weaving. I try to ignore the sounds of his heavy breathing and the scrape of the straw mat on the floor and Sheila's tiny whimpers like a hurt puppy. I must weave flowers. I must weave flowers. I must weave...

He turns on his back and falls asleep. Sheila and I eat the *dal* and rice in silence. After I wash up, I signal her to help me with the flowers. We sit up to 4.00 a.m. till we are done and I fall asleep exhausted.

"Rand!" I hear him shout from far away, blissful he is not here, till I feel the pain in my side. I wake and find him ready to kick me once again. I jump to my feet.

"Where is the money?" he shouts.

I take it from my sari blouse and hand it over silently. He grabs the money and pushes me away. He has dressed early today. He walks out the door and down the road. We watch him disappear and rush back to dress. I tell Sheila to wait at home and finish the cooking while I run to the bazaar with my basket of *venis*. I deliver, take a fresh basket of loose flowers, and run home with the money. I keep the flowers at home and tell Sheila to start weaving them while I go to meet Mother.

She is waiting at the gate. I run to her. She calls for an auto rickshaw and we sit in it. I am proud to be sitting with her. She looks at me and smiles slightly. We go to a studio. She gets the photographer to take my picture and we return to the auto rickshaw. Our next stop is a bank. I feel lost. I feel everyone is looking at me. I walk close behind her. She writes on a paper at the desk and talks to the man in English. They ask me to dip my thumb in the stamp pad and the man takes my fingerprint.

As we come out she says, "You now have a bank account. I have put five hundred rupees in it. You gave me one hundred rupees. You will have to give me back four hundred rupees by saving everyday and then the five hundred will be yours. After that, I will put another five hundred and open a fixed deposit for you. You have to work as hard as you can, and save as much as you can to give me every day. I have your bank passbooks. Do not tell anyone about this."

I nod, excited. She is my angel of hope. Now I have a bank account. She takes the rickshaw up to her building and I run home happy. I forget to ask her how Uncle is. Never mind, I will do it tomorrow. I run to the market and ask for another basket of flowers. We no longer sit and wait for Him. Sheila and I do four baskets a day. We sit up to four a,m. each day and deliver the flowers. I dream of my bank account. I dream of moving to the building where Mother lives. I dream..."

Mother adds Sheila's name to the account. I agree. Together we earn more. We are both very excited. Sheila and I start cleaning the road outside our home. We buy a doormat at the bazaar and put it at the door. We are so proud that we walk around it, not to dirty it with our feet. Sheila no longer cries after he finishes with her in the night. She lies still till he finishes and, once he is asleep, joins me in weaving flowers.

We spend our mornings on the doorstep in the sun, weaving flowers and watching the dogs play and get into gang fights. We watch the mangy leader, who pisses on the neighbour's doorstep every day. We watch the neighbour kick the dog when he sees him pissing. The mangy leader is undeterred nevertheless and pisses on the doorstep everyday.

Our life is full of dreams and hope. Sheila and I work feverishly each day. She listens while I talk of my dreams. She is a quiet little thing, but she looks stronger now. We have a mother, a bank account, and a doormat. Today as we sit on the doorstep resting after a long stretch of weaving flowers, Sheila says,

"*Didi*, shall we go to the garden to play?"

"No, Sheila, you are now a married woman, you cannot play in the park," I say, not quite convinced as I look at this child.

"But *Didi*, why can't a married woman play? Look at those girls. They are your age and they are playing in the garden."

"Yes, but they live in the big buildings. They have different customs. That is not for us."

"Yes, but *Didi*, we are not different. We do not have money but we can play. You do not need money for the games they are playing."

"Sheila, people will talk. He will beat us if we go out to the garden," I tell her, smoothing her hair down on her head.

"*Didi*, we can go to another garden where people do not know us."

"Yes. But what if someone does see us? And how will we walk there and back without affecting our work?" Watching her face fall, I add, "We can play here inside the house."

"What do we play inside the house, *Didi*?"

"OK. Show me how clever you are. Tomorrow we will play a game which you invent," I say placating.

We wait once again on the steps for Mother.

The next day I run to the bazaar to get fresh flowers to weave. When I return Sheila is excited and looks mischievous.

"What?" I ask her.

"I have thought of a game."

"Later," I say, "when we finish our work."

So we feverishly work and she is very excited and full of laughter. I feel happy too, seeing her excitement. I wonder what the game is.

"What is the game?"

"Later," she says mischievously, "after we finish our work."

We weave, we weave, we weave...

"Now," I say, "now let us play," I say curious to see what she has thought up.

"OK, *Didi*, close your eyes."

I close my eyes and wait for a long time before I try to peep from under my eyelashes. She has gone outside and has half shut the door. She knocks.

"Come in," I say.

Sheila walks in, partly staggering, and sticks her chest out comically. She strides around the room and then stands above me while I sit there, wondering what the game is. She turns her skirt to the front to get the string that holds it up. There is an opening the size of my palm between the string and the seam that runs down to the hem of the skirt. She wiggles her bottom a bit and out pops a twig slightly longer than the palm of my hands. She has tied it with a string inside the skirt and now I can only see the protruding twig from the opening at the height of her hips. It is slightly unstable and dangles a bit as she advances upon me, walking in the same style as Him.

She puffs her cheeks, swaying and holding the twig in one hand while she pushes me down with the other. She starts to move but not exactly on my body, allowing me to see what she is doing. She makes noises and then, with a loud "aaaaah," rolls down beside me panting. I laugh. She then stands up and walks to the door holding the twig in one hand and makes a loud "sssssssssssssshhhhhhhhhh."

I run to her and pull her in and close the door so that no one sees her. Once the door is closed, we both collapse laughing and we roll across the floor one over the other, she, me, she, me, laughing and laughing till we hear the dogs bark.

That night as he tortures her with his body she tilts her head and looks at me. I pick up the twig from near my feet and shake it at her. She giggles. This is the first time he hears her laugh.

"Ah, you are growing up! You like this." It is not a question. She glances at me and I shake the stick at her. She laughs and He? I look at his face now. It is smug as he gets up and goes to the door to piss out into the night.

The next day I hang twigs around the house for her to see, no matter what angle she is at when he humps her. The nights are giggles and laughter now till the day, strangely, one thing changes.

He swaggers in, takes Sheila and then me, turns on his back, and falls asleep. We rush to our flowers and weave till four a.m. He is up by six, and pisses on the doorstep. Sheila, now awake, watches him piss. I can see her gulp and hold her mouth. He takes the money I have left on the counter and leaves. As soon as he is out of the door, she rushes and vomits on the doorstep. The retching is severe and I have to hold her. I think it was her retching and the smell of her vomit that set me in motion. I vomit on the doorstep too. We both sit down on the floor after that with tears in our eyes, more from the retching than any real sorrow.

As we collect ourselves, our first thought is the doormat. We both rush to save it. It is reeking with vomit and piss. We take it to the public toilet and wash it thoroughly. We wash ourselves too. We rush back to weave the flowers. To our relief, we do not vomit any more today and are able to deliver the flowers to the bazaar.

In the evening, I tell Mother about it. She nods and says we should both meet her tomorrow at ten. That morning, we watch him piss on the doorstep, take the money and run. This act disgusts us once more. Sheila runs to the door to vomit. I run behind her and grab the doormat to save it. I find the smell of her vomit triggers my nausea too. We sit down panting for a while and then rush to the public toilet, clean up and run to meet Mother. She takes us to the hospital. They give both of us a cup for a urine sample. We oblige and hand it back. Mother then returns us home.

"Mataji, what is wrong?" I ask her.

"Nothing," she says, "we shall soon see."

The next day at noon Mother comes to our home. We are sitting at the doorway weaving flowers.

"Beti," she says, "can we go indoors? I have to talk to you both."

"Mataji, we do not have a chair to offer you."

"That's all right, but I would like to come inside."

We go to our little room. Mataji looks around without saying anything. We wait anxiously for her to speak.

"Both of you are pregnant," she says, smiling.

We look at each other, dismayed. What do we do? How will we manage? Mother is still smiling. She says all is well, not to worry. She gives us two bottles of pills. She says it is iron, so that we are strong to bear the babies. She tells us to eat regularly and gives both of us new saris. We are excited about the saris.

Smiling, she puts her arms over our shoulders and says, "You are both going to be mothers. Always stay happy, no matter what, so that your children will be born smiling. Keep money for them and educate them. They will be your joy."

She leaves. We are excited. Do we tell Him? Sheila says no, I say yes.

He comes home that night heavily drunk. We are too scared to speak. It's the same as usual: fuck, sleep, snore, piss on the doorstep, second fuck, sleep, wake, piss on the doorstep, dress, grab the money, leave.

We vomit, clean, run to the bazaar, and get the flowers home.

"*Didi*," Sheila says.

"Yes?"

"Mataji said to save money for the children."

We silently sit weaving.

"*Didi*, what are you thinking?"

"He will throw me out if I don't give him the money."

We sit in silence, weaving. Our hands do not stop moving and then two hours later, I lie back to sleep. I feel a bit faint. Sheila gets a wet rag, wipes my temple, and puts my head in her lap. It has been a long while since my own mother held me. I have forgotten tenderness. I cry silently inside my heart. The faintness passes and we get back to the work, weaving, weaving, wea…

I don't know what happened. I just felt a sharp pain in my side and whimpered. I open my eyes to find that He has come home early and is getting set to kick me once again. I jump up groggily.

"*Rand*!" he yells, "where is the money?"

"I am not well, I did not sell anything today," I lie.

"Lazy *rand*," he yells, "don't live in this house if you cannot earn." He shoves me and I lose balance. He walks to the door and kicks the doormat.

"Waste of money," he shouts.

The doormat flies down the steps. He stands on the top step and starts pissing. At that moment I hear the long scream and a body flies across the room and shoves him hard. He topples, still holding his penis.

Sheila screams, "Didi, help me," as she stoops down and picks up the smelly doormat. I rush and help her to close the door. Together we lock it. We step to the side and hold each other in fear and suspense. There is going to be hell to pay. We do not know what to do. We stand there waiting.

There is only silence. We sit down on the floor, our legs weak, still holding each other. Nothing happens. We must have fallen asleep for a while because we are both startled by banging on the door. Our fear makes us hold each other tight.

"*Didi, Didi*." It was the neighbour's daughter.

Sheila opens the door. I just sit there, too weak to move.

"*Bhayia*, brother, is fallen out here and hit his head on a rock. I think he is dead!"

He is lying with his pants down, kissing the road. We silently pray that he is. Yes, he is. We both hold each other in relief. The neighbours peer in. They see us just sitting frightened on the floor. The men from the transit camp take his body away. They all contribute for the firewood and cremate him that morning.

Sheila takes the doormat to the public toilet while I run to the bazaar to get flowers to weave . I come back and find the doormat washed and on the doorstep. She is cleaning the house. We both scrub the floor and the walls. We fold his clothes neatly to barter for kitchen utensils. We take the flowers and sit on the doorstep weaving silently till the light fades. We wonder why Mother has not passed today at six.

Early the next day we deliver the flowers to the market. There is an unhurried lightness in our step, a sense of leisure. We get back the fresh flowers, weave and weave, our hands moving in rhythm with the music in our hearts. Our day is like every other, except that the heavy feeling in my chest seems to have disappeared. Today I look forward to meeting Mother. We sit on the doorstep unhurried as the sun moves down in the sky opposite us. At 5.30 p.m. I feel the same customary lilt of expectation that I feel for a full half hour before I see her. At 6.15 p.m. I know she will not pass this way. I know that we must find her.

Sheila and I wear the saris she gave us and go to her apartment. The maid opens the door.

"I don't think she will meet you," she says

"Why?"

"Since Uncle died, she has been silent," she whispers.

"Uncle died?" I feel stupid.

"Two days ago," she says.

"Please let us in," I plead, "we will not talk."

She opens the door wide. Mother is sitting on the balcony looking out.

Silently we sit on the chairs on either side of her. We stare out of the balcony too.

I look at the full moon, which is a faint big ball in the dusk of the sky.

I see our sons walk down the street in the uniforms of the convent school.

I see them in the college opposite Mother's house.

I see them in ties and suits.
I see them in a car.
I see my grandchildren play in the park.
I see the moon now bright in the summer night.

cobras and pigs, holy cow!

*When we really begin to live in the world, then we
understand what is meant by brotherhood or mankind,
and not before.*

~ Swami Vivekanand

LOUISA CASTELLINO SWORE the cobra that sat in her living room had flown in through the window.

"I saw it with my own two eyes," she tells Marie, her neighbour, who knows about these things.

"Go to Fr. Pereira," Marie advises. "He knows."

"Nothing to know man," says Louisa.

"It is that Muslim," she says, wagging her finger towards the empty house. "He said he would not let me be in peace after we evicted him. He has put *najjar*, an evil spell, on us. So we killed the snake."

Marie shakes her head.

"Killed it? Oh My! Holy Mother of God," she says, spreading her arms and rolling her eyes heavenward, "you will be attacked by cobras. The family will come back. Better to go to Caetan. He is the cobra repeller."

Caetan comes the next day. He finds two cobras in the rafters.

"I am cursed," Louisa says.

"Go to Fr. Pereira," Marie, who knows about these things, advises.

Marie goes to St. Francis d'Assisi Church in the next village.

"This is a Muslim curse," Fr. Periera says, "I cannot remove it. Go to Ramdas Muni. He is a powerful Hindu tantric."

Louisa goes to Ramdas Muni. Thank God, he knows how to remove the evil eye.

"Yes, yes, it is a Muslim curse," says Ramdas Muni, "Go dig outside the four corners of your house and you will find four pots buried there. Take them to the river and throw them in."

Louisa goes home and digs up the four corners. She finds the four pots.

Thank God, the Hindu black magic is more powerful than the Muslims'. She throws the pots in the river.

The Castellino property stretches from the road at Derebail market, close to   the centre of town in Mangalore, down a mile south. The pathway to the house is a long strip of elevated land, above the level of the lush paddy fields on one side and a shallow narrow channel on the other, in level with the actual property where the house stands. To get to the house, a little wooden plank on which one balances to get to the other side, bridges the narrow channel (a wohl, as they call it in those parts) that releases water during the rains. When the rain does come, the water billows, and takes with it all that is lying asleep in the wohl: snakes and fish and weeds and fallen branches of coconut trees, empty and rotten coconuts. Sometimes buffalo swim for relief from the heat.

That night the Castellinos go early to bed, like any other day. Within an hour, the Castellino family is snoring in chorus. Franky and Louisa, sprawled across an old rosewood four-poster bed, sing a duet with their noses. Old Rose Castellino slumbers in her room at the back of the house like a squeaky door being open and shut and in the east side of the house Cynthia snorts, while her three kids lie in their bunks fast asleep.

Even the family pig in the sty behind the kitchen heaves rhythmically like a rickshaw driver pressing his horn at a turning in the road. The noises of the Castellino household drown the noises of the night; the small noises of the worms biting into the wooden furniture, the occasional croak of the frogs and the distant sounds of foxes crunching bones in the cemetery.

The air is scented with the faeces of the pig, the flavour of the mango blossoms, and the ripening of the occasional jackfruit. Every once in a while, the dark night lights up with the glow worms on the mulberry tree in the west end of the property touching the little bridge.

It is exactly 11.45 p.m.

OOOOOOOoooo... Louisa wakes up startled and sits upright listening. Is it an owl? Am I dreaming? She shakes her head.

Oooo.. ooo...ooo. There is no mistaking it.

She jumps out of bed and frantically shakes Franky.

"It's an owl. Wake up the family!"

Franky jumps up. This is the most agile thing he has done since he left school twenty years ago. He runs to his sister Cynthia's room and then to her little boys'.

"Quick, quick, come to the compound!" He shakes them awake.

The children blink. John, the youngest, drags his blanket, clutching it, and ambles behind the rest. Louisa runs to her mother-in-law's room. She shakes the snoring frail body and helps her get out of bed.

In the compound the Castellino family stands in fear, holds hands in a circle, and recites in loud excited voices, "I believe, in God the Father, Creator of Heaven and earth" Their voices reach a frightened crescendo, "and life everlasting, AMEN."

In one coordinated movement like a dance, they pick up stones and start pelting it in the direction of the hoots. They hold each other's hands encircling the mango tree. Big-eyed and trembling, they walk around thrice anti-clockwise and repeat the motion clockwise. In their sleepy minds run the images of the owl following their movements and slowly wringing its own neck.

Silence takes over. They bow their heads together and Franky leads the prayer:

Good night, God, we're going to bed,
Work is over, prayers are said,
We're not afraid of night,
You shall watch us,
Till morning light.

Ten minutes later, the Castellino orchestra sets up its melody, undisturbed till the sun is high in the afternoon sky.

That afternoon Louisa finds her mother-in-law dead in her bed.

"She died from natural causes. Old Rose Castellino was old and frail and her heart could not take strain or excitement," says Dr. Cardoza.

Franky goes to the church to inform the new priest.

"It is that Muslim man Ahmed," Louisa says. "He has cursed us."

She goes to Ramdas Muni to take away the evil that is following them.

Ramdas Muni nods wisely.

"Yes, yes, it is the Muslim man. Go and dig under the mango tree."

That is a hard task. The mango tree is huge and at least over twenty years old. Louisa asks Marie to help.

"No, Baba, what if the spirit we release follows me. I do not want to be involved," Marie says.

Louisa sends Franky to the market to hire some labour. Two men, tall and sturdy, come down to the property.

"Don't tell them why," she instructs. "Just tell them to dig around the tree."

The men do not care why. They ask to be paid double.

"These are crazy people," they say, as they dig randomly under the tree.

They find a pot covered with a sieve made of palm leaves as a lid. The smell sends them reeling. They throw a rag over it. Louisa runs indoors screaming.

"Throw it in the wohl, throw it in the wohl."

They carry the pot to the wohl, which still has water flowing through it.

Later that afternoon, two miles away upstream, Susher sits on the wall that borders the school campus where he teaches, and keeps the schoolchildren away from the wohl. Though why protect them he cannot understand. They all jump in and swim. Perhaps it is not to protect them. He knows well that walls do not protect. He looks up at the sky where the Gods sit. The sky seems quiet. And the Gods? They seem to have forgotten him.

Hindustan Vidyalaya, where Susher works, is a "special school." The founders call it "experimental" and it is funded by the government under the "schemes for scheduled caste and scheduled tribes." Susher, who graduated from this school, is the only lower-caste teacher employed here. He understands the principles on which the school was built. The residents accept him, and is grateful for this.

Every morning he stands on his doorstep, bows thrice to the rising sun, and never ventures out during the full moon. Though the school makes light of such customs and beliefs he does not want to take a chance. The others watch him with dismay, hoping that the children from the school do not imbibe such beliefs

The residents have very little to do in their spare time. This is a small town. Konkanee is the oldest woman on the campus; her husband teaches there. Her days are filled with boredom and knitting. Though in her late seventies, she schemes and plans most of the practical jokes on the campus and last night's prank, like most of her pranks, is directed at Susher. She is impatient of his ignorant superstitious mind despite his having spent all his growing years on a campus with liberal-minded faculty.

As she sat at dinner the night before, with her usual band of pranksters who constantly dropped by to eat her wonderful meals, she had a great idea.

"Let us play on Susher's superstitious mind," she announced.

"How?"

She went to her kitchen, brought out a sour lime with five green chillies, and sat down with a needle and twine. She strung the objects together and wrapped them in a muslin cloth. She instructed one of the gang to place it on Susher's doorstep.

Susher steps out at sunrise for his customary sun worship. He breathes in the hot dry air, looking up at the sky and then at the eastern horizon. As the sun peeps over the mango tree in the distance he bends down in worship. His eyes lit on the package on the ground near his feet. He looked like a chicken picked out of a cage who knows his death is at hand.

Susher stands frozen in that bent position for a full five minutes. He forgets that he has not finished his worship and runs indoors and starts rummaging for a dustpan in the cupboard under the sink to pick up the offending object. As he picks up the dustpan, he notices an envelope stuck to the roof of the cupboard. He grabs the dustpan and the envelope. He stuffs the envelope into his pyjama pocket and walks back to the door with a sense of foreboding.

He strides hurriedly to the wohl to throw the object in and then sits on the wall to gather his breath. The crunching noise in his pocket reminds him of the envelope. He pulls it out, and settles down to examine its contents. What he sees in the envelope makes him sick to his stomach. In pain and disbelief, he bends to examine the contents more closely.

The picture of his daughter, in the arms of who he recognises as that stupid Muslim boy, stares back at him. The rat! He reads the letter with its promises of undying love and elopement. Her mother would have known what to do... *I miss my wife. How can I allow my lovely daughter to marry a Muslim? She cannot marry a Muslim. We have so many good Hindu boys. Anybody, anybody, but a Muslim. And not a Muslim named Osama... Oh Ganesha! Give me the strength. Give me an answer. Give me a sign. Tell me what to do.* His gaze moves away from the picture and down into the wohl. As if in reply, he sees a pot covered with a palm-leaf sieve float by chased by a snake. Then suddenly, as if in answer for a sign, the pot tips over, and the sieve and two dead rats pop out. This seems an answer to a prayer of the snake – and Susher. He returns home with a renewed calm.

That night, howling squeals rend the quiet still air. The village continues to sleep undisturbed as if it were part of the noises in their subconscious, the noises of the night: the croaking frogs, yelling cicadas, woodworms, and the fox crunching bones in the cemetery.

In the morning, Ahmed, the Muslim man of Louisa's nightmares, finds the heart and ears of a slaughtered pig on his doorstep. The milk bag and the newspaper on the doorstep is now disguised with coagulated blood. Ahmed calls his wife Munira. They whisper, scared to disturb the children. "A pig? Most definitely the work of a Hindu... Kaffir. Allah strike him! Anyway, we cannot touch it. We will have to find a Hindu."

Munira walks down the street to see her friend Farzana. They both go to Dilshad. Dilshad tells her husband. The Muslims whisper. The village continues in their daily activity. Ahmed goes to his store. Meena, Sita, and Smita from the village buy rice from him. He smiles at them and takes their money. All seems well.

The next morning the villagers passing the temple walk round the cow lying slaughtered on the doorstep. Anand tells Ram. Ram and Anand walk over to Shanker, the Brahmin priest. "It is a sacrilege. We must teach these Muslims. They think they can do whatever they want in our country... just because we tolerate them. They should be taught a lesson."

The Muslim bakery is the first to be burnt down. Then the Hindu paan shop. Then the Muslim abattoir. Then Ahmed gets stabbed. Then Ram. Then Mohammed. Then Lakshaman. Friends bar their doors. Neighbours bar their doors. Amidst the carnage, a quiet purposeful Susher walks to the door of Osama and rings the doorbell. The unsuspecting Osama opens the door. Susher stabs him, saying, "Take that for touching my daughter," then, "and that for even looking at her," and walks away, feeling at rest. He throws the bloody knife in the wohl and goes home.

The morning sun is bright red on the horizon. In the distance, high on the oldest jackfruit tree, a family of vultures sit gossiping. They watch Smita walk into Ahmed's shop. They wonder what is happening inside. They cannot see her nod in silent apology to Munira behind the counter. They cannot hear her ask about Ahmed's absence because she does not.

The temple bells ring and down the street the Imam gives the Azan, calling all the faithful to pray. Mohammed and Lakshaman, the only two constables in the village, try not to look at each other in the ward where they lie recovering. The cowbells and the woodworm resume their little sounds in this quiet town in South India.

The Castellino family sits at lunch that day. Louisa brings out the much-awaited Pork Sorpotel. Franky pours out the toddy. The children wait eagerly for their favourite dish.

Bless us oh Lord
And these thy gifts
Which we are about to receive through Christ our Lord,
Amen.

They tuck into the Pork Sorpotel and Sannas, the rice bread, fermented with toddy.

"Does not taste the same without the heart," Franky says.

The rest of the family pig, cut into little pieces and salted, is out on a coconut leaf mat in the cow-dung compound. It will stay there a few days till all its moisture is gone. It will be then stored in huge, salt-glazed earthen jars, off-white with buff trim on the top.

They will sit in the dark, cool pantry till the monsoons, when fish and meat is hard to come by. They will stay there for a rainy day.

she married a pumpkin

If two lie down together, they will keep warm.
But how can one keep warm alone?

~ Ecclesiastes 4:9-120

SEETHA IS THE prettiest girl in Mohan Nagar. South of the Nagpur Railway station, in the little neighbourhood called Mohan Nagar, the residents hardly ever venture beyond its boundaries except to the movie house. They acclaim that she is by far the prettiest girl in all of Nagpur. All the young men of Mohan Nagar have at one time or other entertained thoughts of marrying her. Dr. Vishnu Paranjape has not given up. He stands at the edge of the crowd and watches the ceremony with the pumpkin.

Mrs. Deshpande is in labour. They want everything to be right. It is their first child and all the traditions have to be maintained. The Pundit enters the delivery room.

"At the first sight of his head I want you to mark the time," Mr. Deshpande says. "This is our first born and it is very important.

"It could be a daughter," puffs Mrs. Deshpande, blowing through her mouth the way the nurse asked her to breathe.

"The Deshpandes have always had sons."

"I want a daughter."

"AAAAh..." Now clearly in pain.

Seetha is born at exactly 11.30 p.m. The Pundit furiously calculates the position of the stars and maps her horoscope. Mr. Deshpande is not very pleased with this upheaval of Deshpande history. Six generations of boys... and now this... It is definitely the fault of his wife's genes. The Pundit shakes his head gravely.

"What?" screamed Mrs. Deshpande in a high pitched nervous voice.

"Nothing," said the Pundit abstractedly.

To the most unlikely of parents is born the prettiest girl in Mohan Nagar. She has a sweet temperament to match and Mr. Deshpande, though disappointed with the birth of a daughter, absolutely adores the little doll. Her manners, her gait, her very sharp mind and, above all, her love of her parents is, if anything, perfect. No effort is spared to please her and Seetha grew up with a sense of wonder about creation itself. So perfect is her life.

Little wonder that so perfect a being should be cherished by the entire neighbourhood, except of course by other young girls, who find the gooey-eyed men a travesty of manhood. They know that it is no fault of Seetha, for she does nothing to encourage men. She just is. Nevertheless, is it not a total injustice in an incestuous neighbourhood to have them gawk at one woman? They wait patiently for Seetha's parents to announce that they are ready to entertain marriage proposals for their daughter.

On her twentieth birthday, not long after Seetha graduates, her mother makes the long-awaited announcement. Everyone is excited. The girls are pleased. Finally she would marry and be unavailable. The young men, holding back for this announcement, will once again be available. The men go home that evening excited. Seetha, as a good, respectable, and obedient girl, had not allowed herself clandestine affairs with any of them. All of them wonder who she will choose.

But Seetha will choose the man her parents will bring. They will have her best interests at heart. Seetha knows they will weed out those that do not suit her and she trusts their intentions and ability to choose the man for her. Seetha's marriage is important to many lives in Mohan Nagar and a little beyond.

The first person to come to her home very early the next day is Vishnu. Dr. Vishnu Paranjape, M.D., from a good Konkanasta Brahmin family, has everything a good proposal is made of. A top Maharashtrian Brahmin family, a doctor earning well, his own house in an expensive part of Nagpur (though austerely furnished), fair, tall —just about everything.

"No," she says, "definitely not. *Ahi*, mother, I don't like him."

"This is a great match," says Mr. Deshpande, quite annoyed. *It is very difficult to have daughters, even pretty ones. I will have done my duty and sooner the better. I hope she is not going to be a choosy girl.* "Get her to agree," he orders his wife.

"She does not want him," his wife says.

"If she turns down such good proposals she will never find a boy."

"She will. Who would not want such a pretty girl? She is loving, obedient, and respectful."

"You have spoilt her. She now feels she has a choice and we will have a really hard time with proposals. Besides, you should have taught her to cook – something she knows nothing about. What will she do in her in-laws' house?"

"We will see that the boy she marries has his

own house."

"Tell her that Vishnu is a good boy," he says, ignoring all she has just said. "Convince her. It is your role as mother, not mine."

"Seetha, beti, my daughter."

"Yes, ahi, mother?"

"You do know we have your best interest at heart?"

"Yes, ahi."

"Your father thinks Vishnu is a very good match."

"And you, ahi? Do you also think so?"

"He has everything a husband of yours should have. Besides, he is used to looking after himself and would help you with the housework."

"Ahi, did you notice his hairline?"

"What about his hairline?"

"It is receding at the temples. He could well be bald by thirty."

"There is nothing wrong with bald men. Your father was bald by thirty-five."

"Yes, ahi, I know he is your husband and my father and I love him. But I don't want someone who looks like my father."

"OK, beti. I want you to be happy. I will tell your father. Besides, I don't think you should say yes to the first proposal you get. You need to have a choice."

"Thank you, ahi. I love you."

"I love you too and so does your father."

Ramesh is a shippee. He would sail eight months of the year and leave my daughter alone. Harish is a business man. What if he incurred losses? It is too risky to marry a business man. Very unstable life she will have. Mahesh's parents are always fighting. It is logical that the son would believe this

to be normal behaviour. We cannot have him in our family.
Naresh had a mentally unstable aunt. Madness is genetic.
Dhananjay is a Maratha. The town was running out of
men. Seetha was unconcerned. Her life with her parents
could not be happier. Marriage would happen. She is
the prettiest girl in Mohan Nagar.

As her twenty-first birthday approaches,
Seetha's life changed dramatically with the inflation in
the real estate market in Mumbai. KPGG Consulting
has just advised Bharat Motor Ltd. on a major restruc-
turing. "Relocate. Relocate your factory to Nagpur. Relocate your corporate office and cash in the inflation.
Vidarbha region is on a growth path. There are many
investment incentives to businesses as well as tax holidays. The company is overextending on wages and pro-
duction costs are lower in a place like Nagpur."

Srikant Pathare, CEO, Bharat Motors Ltd.,
found himself standing outside Nagpur Station with
a briefcase and an overnight bag, waiting for a taxi to
take him to Sitabuldi. It was May and the heat was at its
most extreme. *Forty-five degree Celsius is nearly halfway to*
boiling water. I don't think we should relocate here. Besides
it is going to mess up my social life. He crossed the street
to have a chai at the sweetmeat stall opposite when the
vision he saw transformed Nagpur to the perfect new
home for Bharat Motors Ltd.

Seetha, whose twenty-first birthday is two days
away, had come to the sweetmeat stall to order *barfi* for
the landmark birthday. "Maybe your last birthday with
us," her mother said.

"Who is she?" he asked the stall owner.

"Seetha."

"Alone? Where is her husband?"

"She is single. They are looking for a match for
her."

Yes, of course, KPGG was right about the relocation. This was a good location for any business, he thought.

"*Ad nav kai*? What is her surname?"

"Deshpande."

"Ah, Deshasta Brahmins." Good. This seems perfect.

"Yes. Very good family."

"Where does she live?"

"Mohan Nagar."

"*Kuthe*? Where?

"Opposite the church. Anyone can direct you."

Mr. Deshpande, the teller at the State Bank of India at its main branch in Nagpur, found what he thought was a customer, pushing a business card across his counter. He looked down at the business card and up at the young handsome gentleman. He was impressed. Very impressed indeed. The CEO of Bharat Motors Ltd. had stopped at his counter and actually passed his business card to him.

"How can I help you, sir?" he said, almost servile.

"I would like to have a brief private moment with you, sir."

"Now?"

"If you please, yes, now."

Mr. Deshpande locked up the cash drawer and his little cubicle. He was surprised and unsure why he had been singled out by this very important man. To ensure privacy, he took him to the Accounts Manager's office, which was vacant. A bit concerned, he did not want the subject of their conversation to be known to anyone else in the bank. It could be anything, he thought. He walked in, followed by Mr. Srikant Pathare, CEO,

Bharat Motors Ltd.

"Sir," he said, "please be brief. I have to get back to the cash; else I will have a riot on my hands. As you can see, it is a very busy day."

"Thank you, sir, for giving me your time. I will be brief indeed. I want to marry your daughter."

Mr. Deshpande, taken aback, did not know how to react. Welcome though this was, it was sudden and unexpected.

"We do not know anything about you, sir. Could you tell me where you come from and who are your parents?"

"We are Pathares from Mumbai," Srikant said importantly. "I understand your concerns, sir, and my parents will contact you formally if you agree."

"Please ask your parents to contact me at this number. I prefer that we speak on phone." He slipped his business card to Srikant.

"Can I offer you some tea, sir?" he said, quite forgetting his earlier haste.

"Thank you, sir."

"*Do chai*, two teas," he said to the canteen boy who, passing at this moment outside the open door of the Accounts Manager's office, had just peeped in. Both men, in their respective haste, gulped the steaming sweet chai down tongues' whose sensitivity had long been tested by the pungent food and endless steaming teas that corporate life involved. They stood up simultaneously and shook hands.

"Thank you, sir."

"No. Thank *you*," Srikant said.

Srikant spent most part of the day trying to get his mother on the phone. Relocation will happen, he thinks, but this is urgent and important. After half a day of dialling, he got his mother on the line.

"Son, I know you would miss me," she said.

"Always," he lied.

"And what are you up to there?"

"Mother, do you have a pen and paper with you?"

"Why, son?"

"Do you?"

"Hold on."

At this point the phone lines in Nagpur went dead, along with the electricity. The periodic load-shedding, a way of life here in Nagpur, was unusual for Srikant from Mumbai. He uttered a few choice expletives. Mrs. Pathare, of the Pathares of Mumbai, spent the rest of the day waiting with pen and paper for her son to call. Unfortunately, the phone lines did not oblige.

Meanwhile, Mr. Deshpande fielded the questions the other cashiers asked him. He was not a cricket player. But questions from the curious he fielded with the skill of one.

"Deshpande, who was that?"

"No one you would know."

"What did he want?"

"Oh, he wanted to know how to open a new account."

"Why didn't you send him to the Personal Banking Manager?"

"He came to me. In the interest of good service I did not want to bounce him around."

"But the Personal Banking Manager will feel upset you are encroaching on his territory."

"Oh, he is such a *kam chor*, a slacker, he will be happy I did some of his work."

That silenced his co-workers for a while. Indeed, the Personal Banking Manager was a *kam chor*.

Mr. Deshpande couldn't contain himself. He closed his cash early and wound up for the day. He took his bicycle home, very pensive. I hope my daughter will like this man, he thought. Though I personally would prefer a professional like Vishnu. Her mother spoils her. We could have got her married last year. I will warn her mother not to listen to all her fuss about the proposals. She may be the most beautiful girl in town, but there is a limit to suitable men in this town. I don't even have enough savings to give a large dowry. Vishnu was prepared to marry her without a dowry. These women do not understand commerce. They would if they had to pay, he thought, a trifle bitter about his state of finances.

"We will have to see his background," Mrs. Deshpande said. "And his horoscope should match. And also see what his parents will demand. But he is a CEO and must earn well. Anyway, no need to tell Seetha till all this is settled."

Mr. Deshpande fell silent. This was complicating the issue. Anyway, from experience he knew that his wife would get her own way. Mrs. Deshpande got to work. She dressed up and took the bus to Kamptee to visit her friend Mrs. Agashe. Mrs. Agashe's cousin's wife's brother-in-law was a CEO. She very authoritatively said that a CEO definitely earned a seven-figure salary. Besides, they received huge perks. Mrs. Deshpande went home quite satisfied with her trip.

That night Mrs. Deshpande was the only one who slept well. Srikant, frustrated with the phones, could not sleep. What if she did not want him? He had never seen such a beautiful face. He tossed and turned, impatient and unsure of his future.

Mr. Deshpande was very irritable. While he

wondered how to get his women to be more practical, his wife had started snoring in loud bursts. He would have to get her treated for sleep apnoea, he thought, in between resentment for the woman and concern about her snoring.

Mrs. Pathare sat beside the phone, expecting it to ring any time. She dozed and woke and dozed and woke and dozed till the milk man rang the doorbell early next morning.

At seven a.m. the next day the phone rang. Her son, who had spent as sleepless a night as she, was on the line.

"Srikant," she screamed, thinking the long-distance call made it difficult for him to hear her. "I have a pen and paper ready."

"Mother, please take down this phone number. It is Mr. Deshpande's number. I have seen his daughter and I want to marry her. You will have to talk to Mr. Deshpande about it. I told him you will."

"Son, we have to see the family first."

"Mother, it is a good Brahmin family. They are Deshpandes. No, no. Not CKP Brahmins. These are Deshastas."

"OK, son. But we have to match the horoscopes."

"OK, mother. But please hurry. I don't want to be late. This girl is so good-looking I am surprised she is single."

"How old is she?"

"She looks twenty."

"Son, I will call and ask them to send the horoscope."

"Mother, it'll take a long time by post. Can you come down with the *jyotish*, the astrologer?"

"Son, who'll cook for your father? You know

he can't do without me."

"Bring father along. You have my blank cheques. Go get the cash and come by air."

The Pathares returned to Mumbai two days later. The horoscopes did not match. Srikant said, "I don't care, I want her."

"Maybe, son, but we want you too. We don't want to see you die."

"Mother you know that's all old-fashioned nonsense."

"The girl's horoscope says her first husband will die within a year of the marriage."

"What if they are wrong?"

"What if they are right?"

Srikant Pathare returned to Mumbai.

"No," he said firmly at the board meeting. "Nagpur is not suitable for relocation. We will have to move somewhere closer. Perhaps Pune. Nothing works in Nagpur, the phones, the lights, etc." *And life*, he thought.

It was a shock to the Deshpandes and the rest of Mohan Nagar. The young men began looking around at other young women. The young women looked at Seetha pityingly. The Deshpandes had to think hard. They were no longer the drivers of this marriage engine. For the rest of Mohan Nagar, it seemed like a marriage season — weddings one after the other. All the other young women in Mohan Nagar of marriageable age were getting married.

Seetha discovered an amazing truth. Far from marriage binding you, it freed you to do what you wanted. The young women, the friends of her childhood, walked about town as they pleased, as only married women can. Nobody noticed them or asked questions.

A year later, she discovered that married women have very tiring conversations. They talk about nappies, babies sleep times, cooking recipes, husbands idiosyncracies, all of which are designed to make a single woman feel either excluded or very very bored. Seetha felt both. She no longer got invited to parties her young married friends threw. And at the end of the second year, every last friend married.

Seetha's parents found it increasingly hard to engage their daughter at the family dinner table. It was heartbreaking for them to see their wonderful, innocent, good-natured daughter develop that little bitter curl of her lip. She snapped back especially at Mrs. Deshpande, who was the closest to her. Her father kept at a distance, not knowing what to do.

Nagpur is not a place where you have quick reactions. It could be the heat or the pace or just a way of life. The Deshpandes realized that since the day the flaw in Seetha's horoscope revealed itself three full years had elapsed without a single proposal coming forward. Even that nice Dr. Vishnu Paranjape, who was still single, did not attempt to repeat his offer. Every so often, Mr. Deshpande was tempted to take the voluntary retirement scheme that the bank offered and give a large dowry to Dr. Vishnu if he took his now increasingly unmanageable daughter off his hands.

Mrs. Deshpande finally decided to go on a pilgrimage with Seetha to Tirupathi to ask for answers. She spent most of the time on the journey, sleeping on the upper berth of the train. She could no longer converse with her daughter. She found a very strident, confrontational stranger, with ideas she did not know any young girl from a respectable family could have. Most of their conversations had been like:

"Seetha, come, let me teach you to make chappatis."

"Why can't we eat bread and be done with it?"

"You're father likes chappatis."

"Why doesn't he make his own chappatis?"

"He is a man. Besides he works and brings the money in."

"I work and bring money in."

"Seetha, if you talk like that you will never get a husband."

"If you didn't notice, I am not getting a husband."

At the hotel in Tirupathi, Mrs. Deshpande took out the little piece of paper on which she had jotted the address of a famous astrologer. She looked across at her daughter. She'll have a fit, she thought. Seetha's stopped believing in anything with stars. She even threw out the little fairy wand that I saved from the school play where she was the beautiful fairy princess, just because it had a shiny star at the end of it. I will leave her behind. Such a pity she's become so much of a shrew. Damn the horoscope. I wonder if the Pundit wrote the exact time of her birth. Nothing can be done about that anyway.

She put the paper away.

"Do you want to come to the temple with me right now?" she asked instead.

"No. I am tired."

This was what she hoped for. She walked out the door.

Mrs. Deshpande's visit to the astrologer ended almost as soon it had begun.

He looked at the chart.

"Very easily remedied."

"How?"

"Get her married to a pumpkin and get the first marriage out of the way. She will then be free to marry again without bringing disaster to the man."

"Thank you."

"You can pay one thousand rupees outside at the desk, in cash."

All of Mohan Nagar was invited to witness Seetha's wedding. It was the public message they decided to give that their daughter would once again be a good catch. Seetha, finding she had no say in this, had reached a level of total intolerance of these foolish customs she was subjected to. She sat silent, wondering how to deal with this ridiculous situation. Finally she nodded her head. *They want me to marry a pumpkin? So I will...*

She demanded all the dignity of a bride on her wedding day. The Deshpandes followed their daughter in and out of sari, jewellery, shoe, and undergarment shops. All that a bride should rightfully have, Seetha demanded. She went to the beauty salon and had a pedicure, manicure, waxing of arms, legs, and underarms, and had *mehndi*, henna patterns, done on her feet and hands. She finally demanded that she should be given a special bride present.

Her mother, afraid to displease this suddenly cooperative daughter, asked, "What would you like?"

"A refrigerator."

"But you will be living with us till you get married to a man," she said, puzzled, wondering where the second refrigerator would fit.

"Ahi, if you want me to get married on Saturday, this is absolutely a must."

Mr. Deshpande did not understand why he had to apply to the bank for a consumer loan. *Women! I wish I had a son. No such nonsense.* He took the cheque and went to Sitabuldi to buy a refrigerator.

The wedding was all a bride could ask for. Even a blushing silent husband. Dr. Vishnu Paranjape resentfully stared at the pumpkin sitting on the chair where he felt rightfully should have been his. How could she agree to this, and not to his suit? He did not want a dowry, did not care for horoscopes, and would have died happy even if it was the first year, satisfied to have married her. He knew deep down that he was not being truthful, because his mother would have demanded the horoscope. He stood there watching her with hope in his heart.

Being a married woman is wonderful - especially when your husband is in the refrigerator. The Deshpandes soon learned that their very cooperative daughter had decided that she enjoyed being a married woman and would like to stay one. They had no control over her whereabouts. She walked through the town with the *sindur*, the vermilion spot on the forehead of married women, and a *mangal sutra*, the black-and-gold beaded necklace symbolic of marriage. She shopped and went to the movies alone.

"Ahi, I am married," she responded to any control on her movements. They questioned themselves on the wisdom of their actions. She even flirted with the husbands of her friends, who had always found her attractive. Mr. Deshpande knew that urgent measures were called for when he found her in a small tea place in Sadar, not far from Mohan Nagar with Harish, her best friend's husband. She is out of control, he thought. She refuses to meet with suitors, saying she is married. She does not let us go near the pumpkin, which is wrapped in cling film and sits prominently inside the marriage gift. The refrigerator had been moved to her room and is off bounds. He winced at the thought of the consumer loan he took out to buy it.

The next morning, he went to the M.S. Patel Cooperative Credit Society for bank employees and applied for a loan. He had to get her out of the way. The Deshpandes dressed that evening in all their finery and went to meet Dr. Vishnu Paranjape.

"Good evening. Are you ill?"

"No," Mr. Deshpande said, in fact feeling quite ill thinking of the loan that would take him several years to repay. "We are here to offer you our daughter's hand if you're still interested in her." He felt humble.

"Does she want this?"

"What's that got to do with anything? I'll give you a large dowry for her. You won't have problems with horoscopes now that the *panvati*, bad luck, is out of the way."

"She said no to me a few years ago."

"She was young and didn't know her mind."

"How do you want to proceed?"

"Maybe your family can dine with us on Saturday."

"That will not be possible. My parents live in Amravati. But I'll call them here. Will next Saturday be OK?"

"Yes, of course," they said, relieved. This seemed like an answer to a prayer.

"I'll bring my aunt and uncle too. My parents will expect them to be there."

"They are welcome."

Seetha sat quietly with her own thoughts as the Deshpandes outlined their plans for Saturday. Vishnu might be a potential bald man, but he was loyal, she thought. The other men had deserted her like rats. She felt warm towards this man. She knew all these past years that he refused to consider any other woman in his life. She appreciated that. But what was all this? Mother, father, uncle, aunt? A *Vadu Pariksha*, a bride test? Now her mother wanted her to read the *Kal Nirnay*, Farmer's Almanac, to prepare for the questions he might ask her! The bitter curl of her lip returned. Why can't I ask him questions? What has general knowledge to do with marrying me? I don't need this. She now began to grow apprehensive they might reject her.

On the Friday before the dinner she announced, "Come with me."

Her mother followed her to her room. As a man, Mr. Deshpande decided not to go along. She opened the refrigerator and pointed to the eight-month-old pumpkin on the bottom shelf of the refrigerator, still looking fresh.

"I take my vows seriously," she said in a final tone. "Besides, I leave for Mumbai tomorrow."

"What! Why?" Mrs. Deshpande stared dismayed at this strange daughter. She could not understand her.

"I promised myself that when I marry I will take a trip to Mumbai to see Sharoukh Khan."

"Sharoukh Khan is a movie star. He will not see you. Besides, where will you stay?"

"I will see where he lives." She ignored the latter part of the question.

"What will your father say?"

"I am married now and not his responsibility."

The next day, Mr. Deshpande carried Seetha's

bags to the station. He knew by now that nothing would stop his daughter. They will have to think of a way. She has carried the pumpkin marriage too far.

He went to the market and collected the long list of items his wife asked him to get. He put down the bags in the kitchen and asked her what the menu would be. They stood looking at each other for a long moment, silent, with one thought in their heads.

The dinner was a huge success. Vishnu arrived with his parents and his maternal aunt and uncle. "You marry families," his mother had always said. They looked around the Deshpande's living room as they greeted each other.

"Where is the girl?" Mrs. Paranjape asked.

"Seetha is very shy and will not come out of her bedroom," Mrs. Deshpande lied.

Ah, modest. My son has chosen well.

"She should not be shy of us. We are going to be family."

"Yes, of course. I am sure she will get over it. But she has cooked all the food for tonight."

It was a splendid meal. Impressed, Mrs. Paranjape looked at the scooped up half-pumpkin filled with Russian salad. *Innovative girl.* The *poha*, the *varan*, stuffed green peppers, the *raita*, and even the mashed pumpkin side dish was delicious. She looked at her son's plate. The untouched pumpkin side dish told a different tale. *This pumpkin is really delicious. Pity Vishnu does not like pumpkins. Funny, I don't remember this when he was a child. Must be a new development. Anyway, she will cook other things or he will just develop a taste for pumpkins.*

"Let us set a date."

A week later, Seetha returned to Mohan Nagar. Mumbai

had been disappointing. She did not get to see any film actors and it was dirty, crowded, and rude. It was good to be back. She stopped the rickshaw on the street and walked to the house. As she entered through the gate, her shocked eyes lit upon the half-pumpkin rotting in the refuse pit. She rushed up to her room.

The stars don't lie. There was a quarter of the huge pumpkin lying desolate in the otherwise empty fridge.

Seetha is the prettiest widow Mohan Nagar ever had.

the guest at my grandfather's house

Athiti devo bhav.
(Treat your guest as God).

~ Veda

WE STAND ON the edge of grandfather's property in Mangalore, watching the villa on the hill, waiting for something to happen. The villa has captured our imagination ever since we were banned from going anywhere near it.

"Why, mummy?"

"Anna, don't ask questions, just don't do it."

So we wove stories around it. Some involved ghosts and some crime and none of them were anywhere normal. The night cries of foxes that sometimes visited our chicken coup always originated from the villa of our minds. This was a large part of our summer holidays in our grandfather's house. Torturous long days away from our friends in Bombay, no one to play with, no library, no books and no newspaper. No radio, no music, just frogs and cicadas who deafened us with their noise; and leave me alone in a room with a cricket bat and the man who first said birds sing!

This was no different a morning. We woke, had coffee sweetened with coconut jaggery. My uncle had already left with the buffalo to plough the fields and we left our dad mending all things broken in the house and property to stand and stare at the villa. My cousins, not allowed to play with us city folk, who clearly had no sense of responsibility and might give them a taste for play, stood at a distance, watching us longingly. Finally, on the quiet hillside we see the tall dark figure through the trees. As he approaches us from over the hill, bouncing down the way people do when they climb down the hill, we recognize Paulo.

Paulo's visit is always the best part of the holidays. As he approaches, we see his bright white shirt with curry stains near his heart and striped blue boxer-style shorts drooping around his knees. I don't know who he is. We all want to know.

"He is a homeless beggar, Anna," my mother said when I was little. "He lives from home to home, a week at a time, wherever he is welcomed and fed and allowed to sleep."

"Is he related to us, mummy?"

"No, Anna. We do not know his family, nor are we related."

So Paulo visited, and lived with village families who would house him. Though he is homeless, Paulo is not humble and we are not patronizing. We are always excited to have him with us. We watch him, getting increasingly animated, from bored to joyous children who welcome a benevolent uncle.

"Paulo, are you coming to our house?" we ask hopefully.

"Yes." He smiles.

We dance and sing to the tune of "Sugar in the morning, sugar in the evening…"

Pauloo in the morning,
Pauloo in the evening
Pauloo at supper time….

We skip on ahead of him, screaming on the top of our voices, "Mummy, Daddy, Paulo is coming here!"

We are hushed into the inner rooms of the house.

"Children should not be in the same room when adults are talking," my dad says. I resent the "children" bit, and don't want to hear the end of his next sentence, "In our day…."

The house has a *sopo*, a verandah that is more like a room running the length of the house. The *sopo* opens out into the inner rooms through doors and one can also look into the *sopo* from the inside through the windows that open out on to it. The wooden-beamed roof is covered with Mangalore terra cotta tiles and held up by round pillars with a design at the bottom. Each pillar is joined by a low concrete patterned wall , which we either sleep on or sit to cool ourselves from the summer heat. Crude fans matted with coconut palms relieve us from the heat and the flies. On such a wall, Paulo sits, one leg over the other, fanning himself as my aunt runs to the kitchen to pour him cool water from an earthen pot.

We madly scramble for the prime place at the windows looking onto the *sopo*.

"How are you?" My aunt hands him a glass of water.

"I am well, and you?"

Today dinner is early. "Get the children to bed," my dad orders my mother. Annoying, annoying, annoying. I am sixteen! We are fed and mother says the night prayers with us. She is in a hurry, too. She does not want to miss out on the scene being played outside. Once she's gone, we run to stand once again at the windows watching Paulo. They are going in to dinner. I crawl into the kitchen at the side of the dining room and the *sopo*.

"Where are you coming from?" my dad asks Paulo.

"I was in Lawrie's house." Everyone is rapt, waiting for more.

"Lawrie and his wife Maggie were fighting once again. Today she did not cook because she was angry with him. So I left. I am not her husband. If she wants to starve him there is no reason why I should starve too. So I left."

The others nod approval.

"Why was she angry with him?" My aunt, were she not illiterate, would make a good investigator. She never gets sidetracked.

"*Sood Kothru,*" he says briefly.

I am familiar with the phrase. I am the Sood Kothru of our family. In this quiet village in Mangalore, Shakespeare had found its way into their language. Sood Kothru, Katherine the Shrew, was used for all sharp-tongued women.

"What did Lawrie do to make her so angry?" my aunt persisted.

"She thinks he is running after Flory, who makes *beedis,*" Paulo says, as he lights his *beedi* and begins to puff at it.

"He thinks he is Lord Falkland," my aunt says.

"Oh, oh, she is no less. She struts around like Madame Pepita," my uncle snorts.

Whoever Madame Pepita and Lord Falkland were, they do not sound popular in this village. Mother spots our faces flattened against the grills and the conversation suddenly flows into Kannada, which we neither speak nor understand. There is nothing to be gained now. Tomorrow. Tomorrow, I will get Paulo alone, I promise myself before I fall asleep.

The myth of a quiet village is broken early with the cock crowing, the buffalo groaning, did I mention birdsong earlier? My uncle leaves for the fields with the plough and the buffalo. They walk through the *wohl*. My aunt takes the pail to milk the she-buffalos and my mother sits with a book. My father pulls out a broken chair from the attic and starts hammering nails into it.

The other children walk to the edge of the property to look up at the villa and I creep up silently on Paulo. We have played this game every time I am here on vacation, ever since I was three. He pretends not to see me. I sit behind him and ask questions of the oracle.

"Why does it rain?" I asked when I was three.

"The gods weep. They see you steal the cashew nuts from the villa on the hill."

I was impressed by the answer. No one had seen me creep up there. Not even the owner. On occasion, he was seen in the village in a hat, sunglasses, well-fitting trousers, smart shirts, the best dressed man in the village. It was rumoured that he was the wealthiest man in the community and far beyond. He never spoke to anyone, nor had anyone ever been to the villa. Our parents had warned us not to enter his property.

"Who is he, mother?"

"No one knows," she said. "See that you don't go there."

Even Paulo had not much to say about him.

"Leave him alone," he said.

So he was left alone. The cousins who lived in my grandfather's house said that the lights did not go on there for many weeks and sometimes months.

I have spent many vacations looking up at the villa. This year I decided to find out. I'd seen the owner only once in all my sixteen years. I was eight.

For a moment, from his gait, I thought it was Paulo. Of course it could not be him. This was a well-dressed man-about-town. Difficult to see his face under the hat and sunglasses. He disappeared, here now, gone in an instant.

"Paulo."

"Yes, Sood. What do you want?"

"Paulo, who lives in the villa?"

"Tomorrow, my child. I will answer tomorrow."

The next morning Paulo had left and my question remained unanswered.

This time he will not evade me.

"Pssst," I say from behind.

"Yes?" says Paulo.

"Answer me, please?"

"What do you want to know, *putha*, child?"

"Tell me about the villa on the hill."

"Tomorrow, child."

"You know I am not a child anymore. I won't forget my question. Tell me Paulo. Pleeese."

"Sood, you know that the topic is off-limits."

"Yes, but you can tell me. I can keep secrets."

"Like the *toran*, raw mangoes, secret?"

"I was eight Paulo." Paulo is referring to the time we went to the mango orchards around the villa. We both gathered the raw mangoes and took it home. "Our secret" Paulo had said. I was excited. When Dad saw the plunder, he asked where I got them from. "Our orchards," I lied. Dad knew I could not have got it from our trees. "Kneel down and say three Hail Mary's as penance for your sin," my father said. Then I turned and pointed to Paulo.

"Dad, he should kneel down too. He took me

there. He stole too."

Dad looked at Paulo. "You are worse than a child," he said. "Take care what you teach them."

"Please, Paulo I was only eight. I can keep secrets."

"Anyway, I don't know much."

"Paulo," I plead, "I don't believe there is anything you don't know in this village."

"Some things I don't know, *putha*, child, but that you were peeping into the windows of the villa last week I certainly do know!"

"There. Now that, no one knew!" I say triumphantly, as though proving my point.

"Ah, ahhh!"

"Tell me, Paulo. Pleeese. I have been waiting for you and I go back to Bombay in a week. Pllleeese."

"Child, let me rest."

"Paulo, you *are* resting. Talking to me should not stress you. Please, Paulo, I may not see you again. I go to college next year and may not take holidays with the family any more."

"Well ok pesky child, what do you want to know?"

"Who lives up there?" I say, pointing in the general direction of the villa.

"Pedro."

"Who is Pedro?"

"No one knows. He is a stranger to this town."

"Why does he not talk to us?"

"He wants to be private."

"Then why does he live in our village if he does not want to talk to us?"

"Not every one who lives in a village needs to talk to each other. Sometimes there are exceptions."

"Does he have a family?"

"Child, this is none of your business."
"Please, Paulo, I won't tell anyone."
"OK, pest. This is the story."

*Pedro was born to a very rich family in a town about hundred
kilometres from here. He was a very naughty child, like you.*
"I'm not."
*Whatever. Anyway, he did not study, skipped school,
vandalized the neighbours' farms, and this and that.*
"So he has a family?"
*Had. His home was an unhappy one. His father beat
him on a regular basis with a stick broom. He just got worse.
Then one day when he was about your age, a neighbour came
to complain about him. Pedro had stolen his mangoes.*
"You and I stole his mangoes, Paulo. Perhaps it
is just a flow of justice."
*Do not justify bad deeds, child. Justice is not meted
out by men but by the universe. There is a natural balance in
nature child. His loss may be justice for his acts, but our gain
is theft. Anyhow, he paid severely.*
"He paid for the mangoes?"
*No, child, it is a manner of speech. That night, after
the neighbour left, his father picked up the stick broom and
advanced on him. Pedro was now a young strapping lad.
He was not going to let his father humiliate him with a stick
broom. He sucked in his stomach and let out the last breath of
air in his lungs, then took a deep breath and rushed towards
his father. The now much older man, so taken by surprise,
let go the broom as Pedro grabbed it and threw it far into the
dung courtyard. It landed with a loud thud, but not louder
than the thud of the old man falling into a wooden chair, that
tipped over only to be stopped by the wall behind.*
"Paulo, my father would throw me out of the
house if I did that."
He did. He recovered his balance and rocked back

the chair to position. Pedro, now quite shocked with his own boldness, ran out not turning back. He could hear the scream that followed him: "Don't come back."

"Where did he go?"

He walked to his grandfather's house, which was about fifty kilometers away. His grandfather was old and hard. He did not like stubborn vagrants even if they were related to him. He refused to take him in. You hit your father today. Tomorrow you will hit me, he said. So Pedro gave up. He did not believe that anyone would take him in especially since he had pushed his father. So he walked down the road and sat at the side of a property which was being dug up, hungry and tired and quite alone. He soon fell asleep.

Early next morning he woke to bright sunshine and birds singing. There was chatter and a very important looking man with a suit coat and a dhoti, walked up to him.

"You are trespassing."

"Sorry."

"Where do you come from?"

"Karkala."

"What are you doing here?"

"I am looking for work."

"How old are you?"

"Twenty," he lied.

"OK, you are on church property. They are building a church here. I am the contractor. Will you work as labour?"

"Yes. I am good. I worked on my father's farm."

"Who is your father?"

Pedro knew that by now the news of his bad deeds could have traveled. He did not take a risk. He lied.

Paulo now started slowly rolling his beedi. He took the dried leaf and wiped it carefully. Then he put a bit of tobacco on it and slowly rolled it up. He tied it with a pink string to hold it together and used a sharp metal instrument to push in the bits of tobacco that peeped out from the ends. Paulo knew he would not lose his audience. He never told a story in a hurry. I looked out of the *sopo* towards the hill. I could not see the villa from here, but it was imprinted in my mind. A lonely man with a sad tale. I sighed. Paulo had an irritating way of making people wait for him. His unhurried manner, as if there were nothing else in the world but that moment to be lived, his distant eyes, and his wonderfully soulful voice - a recipe for impatience.

"Paulo," I said, "He lied. That is where you stopped."

Pedro was hired as a worker on the construction site. He thought of his home but never did get the courage to return. He wiped them out of his memory and his life. He never went back. Not even the thought of Annette the girl he hoped to marry took him back. He knew he had no hope without a home or a family to be an acceptable match for her. He continued to work on construction sites till one day his entire life changed.

"Anna, time for bed." Mother had this way of ordering our lives at inconvenient times.

"Paulo, quick, tell me what happened."

"Tomorrow."

That night I tossed and turned. My dreams of Pedro catching me steal his mangoes and beat me with a stick broom soon changed to Paulo holding my hands and taking me into the woods, telling me the names of the trees and the insects and pointing out to the shapes of the leaves that revealed their identity.

Another day, another long wait for Paulo. We sit on the *sopo* once again and Paulo looks kinder, nicer, more welcoming. I am his stalker. He loves my attention and adoration and takes out a gold sovereign and puts it in my hand.

"Can you keep a secret?"

"Yes."

"This is a lucky coin. Keep it safe. Don't part with it. Don't show it to anyone."

"OK, Paulo, what happened to Pedro. How did his life change."

You see that coin I gave you? That was the way people saved their money in the past. They did not put it in banks. They took their gold coins and put it in a pot and buried it in hidden places. If they kept it at home it could get stolen. Sometimes they buried it under their homes and sometimes in their property. Often times they were so secretive about it that if they died without revealing the spot, their families died in poverty though there was a great deal of gold buried in their very back yards.

"What happened to Pedro?" I think sometimes Paulo goes on these tangents and needs to be brought back.

One day, Pedro being the only homeless worker, was sent to a property far from any habitation. There was a dilapidated house that needed to be pulled down. The new owner wanted a new modern house. Pedro was sent to dig up the ground around and demolish the house.

He started with the outside pillars. He figured that if he weakened the pillars it would bring the house down without much effort. He worked on the opposite pillars first so that the house could implode. It took him over a week to do this. He worked on this alone.

As he started on the third pillar, he felt his pickaxe hit metal. He kept digging and unearthed a large bronze thondor, a big pot for steaming sannas, idlis and other such rice breads.. He tried to open it but found its lid airtight and difficult to open. He tried to lift it and take it to the little shed where he slept at the construction site. It was too heavy.

He found a rope and tied it to the handles and dragged

the thondor *along the ground to the shed. He continued digging and decided to stop early to open the* thondor.

Closer to the end of the day he tied one end of the rope to one of the beams of the shed and then ran the other end through both the handles. He threw the end over the beam and pulled on the rope till the thondor was above the ground. He used his free hand and swung the thondor till it rocked with its own momentum. When the momentum had reached a high swing, he let go of the rope. The thondor swung and fell with a loud ringing and burst open.

The burst of the thondor was like a burst into a new life. Splattered all over the shed were gold coins, very like the one I just gave you.

"Paulo, I have read fairy tales and this is no different."

True. It was a fairy tale for Pedro. Suddenly his life changed. He put it back in the thondor and went to town. He knew he needed a place to hide the coins. He went to the lawyer and told him he wanted to buy the property he was working on.

The lawyer looked at Pedro and told him not to waste his time. Pedro slipped him a gold coin. He said he would give him ten gold coins for the services. He wanted confidentiality. The lawyer settled the deal. The new owner was happy with the appreciation of his property. He did not expect that it would happen so quickly.

Pedro was painstaking. He built his house slowly so as not to arouse suspicion. People who saw him working on the construction site did not associate him with the ownership. But he knew that he could not live there and yet enjoy his wealth freely. Also he had unfinished business. He returned to Karkala to marry Annette. He stayed in a small lodge on the outskirts. But he returned the next day. Annette had married someone from Bombay and left Karkala.

He felt depressed. He kept the house but he moved.

He bought that villa on the hill. He has lived a very successful life. He opened several tile factories and other construction businesses. But he never visits these companies. He deals through his lawyer who knows where he is at all times.

"What a sad fairy story. Paulo. Why didn't he marry someone else?"

"It is about faith, putha. Rejection is a very hard thing. Especially from family. You may want to have a family but you never take that step."

"Where is your family, Paulo?"

"You are my family. My home is where I am and my family is the people I live with."

"I am your family, Paulo," I say, hugging him.

Fifteen years later, I stand outside the villa wondering what to do with it. I meet with Pedro's lawyer tomorrow. I don't understand why I have been named in Pedro's will. I have never met the man. I don't want to live here.

As I sit waiting for the lawyer, I ponder over all the summers I spent in my grandfather's house. Boring, boring, boring, except for Paulo. I will have to dispose of the villa. I could never live here.

"You have been left the villa and enough assets to support you and maintain the villa. The rest has been donated to charity."

"How much are the assets?"

"One crore, ten million rupees in bonds and real estate."

"That is a lot of money."

"Yes."

"I have never met the man. Why did he name me? I did not think he knew of my existence."

"He said you were the only family he had."

"That is impossible."

"He said you were the only one who embraced him and called him family."

"Never met the man."

"You did. You called him Paulo. His real name Pedro was only used in official documents."

"Paulo was a homeless beggar. He lived and moved from house to house in our village. Pedro lived up at the villa."

"Same man."

"Why?"

"Family. He missed family. He wanted to be with family. He figured that it was the only way he could."

I sit in Paulo's chair at the villa. I can hear him say, "Take that leap of faith, *putha*. We all need family."

"This is true and it happened. This is a story of family, community, war and strife. A story of common people deprived of their rights, of bravery and a world they built for themselves."

The storyteller picked up his garment in one hand and raised the other high above his head.

"And so the story is told. By me to you, and my father before me, and his father before him. And so it shall pass down forever; to be remembered till there is equality or till there is life itself."

ACKNOWLEDGEMENTS

My thanks to my friends Shekhar, Philomena and Avita, who made this physically possible and who I am afraid may not know how deeply grateful I am to them.

To my friends at the High Park Library Writers Group, who patiently listened and commented on my work, thank you. To friends whose opinions on my writing I most value, more specially Stephen Kristan, Reva Stern, Herb Ware, thank you.

My special thanks and appreciation to Austin Clarke for his insightful and illustrious foreword.

Many many thanks to my aunt Hilda, whose constant stories sparked ideas as I wrote.

A big thank you to Fr. Kozar, who has constantly provided help in various forms.

I have benefited greatly from my publisher, Bookland Press, who moved this project forward and my editor, Fraser Sutherland, who worked on taking it to the next level.

Above all, to my mother, who gave us the wonderful family that I am a part of, and who is a constant and abiding support to all that I do, my everlasting gratitude.

ABOUT THE AUTHOR

Dr. Jasmine D'Costa was born in Bombay, India and moved to Canada in 2004. As a PhD and international banker for 25 years, Jasmine was published in many academic journals, business magazines and books on international relations, trade, investment, corporate finance and banking. In Canada, Jasmine D'Costa has pursued a career in writing. She now lives in Toronto and brings to the Canadian writing landscape an arresting new voice and her unique gift of nonpareil multicultural storytelling.

Jasmine D'Costa is currently the President of the Writers and Editors Network. *Curry is Thicker than Water* is her first book.

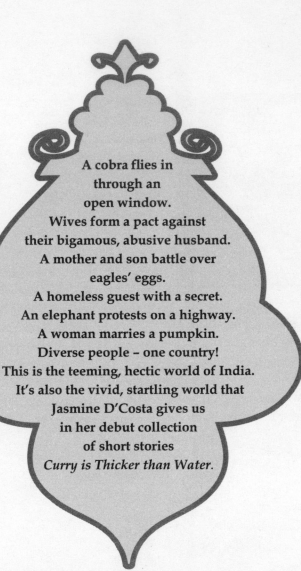

A cobra flies in
through an
open window.
Wives form a pact against
their bigamous, abusive husband.
A mother and son battle over
eagles' eggs.
A homeless guest with a secret.
An elephant protests on a highway.
A woman marries a pumpkin.
Diverse people – one country!
This is the teeming, hectic world of India.
It's also the vivid, startling world that
Jasmine D'Costa gives us
in her debut collection
of short stories
Curry is Thicker than Water.